PUFFIN BOOKS

# THE ADVENTURES OF THE RAILWAY CAT

Alfie is a smart cat who likes to think for himself, but it's a hard life being a railway cat when no one wants you around.

The stories of Alfie, the railway cat, have enchanted young readers ever since they were first published and now, for the first time, all four stories can be found in this one-volumed Puffin edition: *The Railway Cat*, *The Railway Cat and Digby*, *The Railway Cat's Secret* and *The Railway Cat and the Horse*.

Phyllis Arkle was born and educated in Chester, but since 1959 has lived in the Thames Valley village of Twyford in Berkshire. She is actively interested in the Women's Institute movement, and does voluntary work in her village in addition to writing and reading. Her other interests include music and bridge.

# The Adventures
of the
Railway Cat

PHYLLIS ARKLE

Illustrated by Lynne Byrnes

PUFFIN BOOKS

PUFFIN BOOKS

Published by the Penguin Group
Penguin Books Ltd, 27 Wrights Lane, London W8 5TZ, England
Viking Penguin, a division of Penguin Books USA Inc.
375 Hudson Street, New York, New York 10014, USA
Penguin Books Australia Ltd, Ringwood, Victoria, Australia
Penguin Books Canada Ltd, 2801 John Street, Markham, Ontario, Canada L3R 1B4
Penguin Books (NZ) Ltd, 182–190 Wairau Road, Auckland 10, New Zealand

Penguin Books Ltd, Registered Offices: Harmondsworth, Middlesex, England

*The Railway Cat* (1983), *The Railway Cat and Digby* (1984),
*The Railway Cat's Secret* (1985) and *The Railway Cat and the Horse* (1987)
first published by Hodder and Stoughton Children's Books
Published in one volume in Puffin Books 1990
1 3 5 7 9 10 8 6 4 2

Text copyright © Phyllis Arkle, 1983, 1984, 1985, 1987, 1990
Illustrations copyright © Hodder & Stoughton Ltd,
1983, 1984, 1985, 1987, 1990
All rights reserved

Printed in England by Clays Ltd, St Ives plc
Filmset in Linotron Plantin

# CONTENTS

# The Railway Cat

# Contents

# 1

# Alfie Has His Breakfast

A high-speed train rushed – Swooo . . . oo . . . osh! – through the local station. In the waiting room Alfie stretched himself in his basket and yawned. That would be the overnight express to London, so it must be about half-past five, he thought. He snuggled down again, glad to have a nice warm bed on such a cold, wintry morning. It wouldn't surprise him if snow fell before very long.

A quarter of an hour or so later, a freight train chugged through the station and Alfie knew it was getting-up time. No use being the railway cat if you couldn't be on duty before the rest of the staff.

Staff – that reminded Alfie. The last two days Hack, the new Leading Railman, hadn't given him his early morning saucer of milk and half-tin of cat food. It was just too bad! Alfie hoped for better luck this morning, otherwise he might be forced to prowl round the village doorsteps in search of a bottle of milk to knock over. But he didn't want to do that.

A leap on to a bench, a quick jump, a scramble

through a partly open ventilator and the handsome grey and white striped cat was on the platform.

He ran up the steps to the footbridge, which took him over the lines. (He was far too wise to cross any other way.) He arrived on platform 1 just as Hack was putting the key into the lock of the staff-room door.

Alfie followed the man into the room.

'Hello, nuisance, you here already?' was Hack's surly greeting.

'Miaow! Miaow! Miaow!' cried Alfie, as he weaved in and out of the man's legs.

'Well, you can scramble. Be off!' cried Hack. 'I've no time for spoilt cats. Platforms must be swept.' Off he strode to collect a broom.

Alfie was aghast. Sweep the platforms, indeed! What about his, Alfie's, breakfast? Was a cat expected to keep the station clear of mice, *and* be friendly to passengers on an empty stomach? He had feared from the start that there was something unpleasant about this new man.

Swish! Swish! Swish! heard Alfie. He peeped round the door. Hack was taking quick sweeps with a large broom and – with a glance round now and then to make sure no one was looking – pushing the rubbish on to the railway lines.

12

Might have known! thought Alfie. What a way to sweep a platform! Where's his shovel? Too lazy to go and get it, I suppose.

From outside the station came sounds of Splutter! Plop! Splutter! Plop! Ah, good – that would be Fred, the Chargeman, arriving on his scooter. Right on time as usual. Alfie rushed out to meet his friend.

Fred bent down and tickled Alfie under the chin. Alfie enjoyed this but he didn't, as usual, roll over on his back for more. Lack of food and drink was making him feel rather wobbly.

'Miaow! Miaow! Miaow!' he cried, in what he hoped was a mournful tone.

Fred gave him a puzzled glance. 'Alfie seems a bit off colour this morning,' he said to Brown, the Booking Office Clerk, who had just arrived.

'I thought he wasn't quite himself yesterday,' said Brown as he stroked Alfie.

'Well, I'll have a look at you as soon as possible, Alfie,' Fred promised, 'but duty calls at the moment.'

Most of the passengers arriving for the first train were commuters to London. Alfie knew all the regulars. He strolled about accepting a stroke from one, a rub behind the ears from another and a tickle on the chest from yet another.

He noticed a tall stranger standing next to Hack on

the platform. Alfie sat down between the two men. Always get to know the passengers was his motto.

'How are rehearsals going, sir?' Alfie heard Hack ask the man.

'Oh, not bad, not at all bad,' was the answer. 'Expect

we'll manage somehow to be ready for opening night just before Christmas.'

Ah, 'rehearsals', thought Alfie. The man must be an actor working in London for the Christmas season and lodging in the village. Alfie knew several actors, living locally, who regularly used the London trains. The London train drew up at the platform. Doors were opened, passengers crowded in and the doors were slammed. The guard gave a signal and the train moved off.

Next, school children, their breath steaming in the cold air, hurried on to the platform and Alfie had a busy time running from one to the other. He always divided his attention equally as he didn't approve of having favourites. The children waved to him as he ran the full length of the platform alongside the outgoing train.

More local trains arrived and departed and, frequently, express trains thundered through the station. It was nearly ten o'clock before things quietened down, and by that time – my goodness! – Alfie was hungry. He began to feel sorry he'd chased away all the mice! Surely Hack wasn't going to neglect him *again*? The man was nowhere in sight.

But help was at hand.

'Now, let's have a look at you, Alfie,' said Fred. He bent down and carefully pressed his hand over Alfie's back and legs. 'No injured bones,' he declared. Then he gently opened Alfie's mouth and peered down his throat. 'Can't see anything wrong there either.'

Alfie gave his most pathetic, 'Miaow!' and ran off towards the staff room at the end of the platform. He stopped and turned round twice to make sure Fred was following. The staff-room door was open. In went Alfie. He sat down and gazed at an empty saucer on the floor.

'What's this?' said Fred as he picked up the saucer, 'This is *dirty*! It hasn't been used recently.' He put his head round the door and yelled, 'Hack!'

Hack sauntered over. (Oh, don't hurry! thought Alfie.) 'Why didn't you give Alfie his milk and food this morning?' asked Fred.

'No time for cats,' muttered Hack as he shuffled his feet and glared at Alfie.

'Well, you listen to me, Hack,' shouted Fred, his face red with annoyance. 'I'm boss here and *there's always time for Alfie*. Got that? He's one of the staff. *I* feed him in the evenings and *you* do the same in the mornings. Don't forget again. Give him some milk now – in a clean saucer – and food.' Off went Fred in a huff.

Well satisfied at the turn of events, Alfie watched as Hack, mumbling to himself, poured some milk into a clean saucer and placed it on the floor. While Alfie lapped noisily at the milk, the man took a tin of cat food

out of a cupboard – and at last the railway cat was served breakfast.

Soon Alfie felt like a new cat. He diligently licked himself all over, and then gave his ears and long shiny whiskers – not forgetting the spiky hairs above his eyes – an extra wash with his paws.

Ready for any emergency now, he said to himself, as he stepped on to the platform. He growled, 'Brr . . . brr . . . brr . . . .' at Hack as he ran between the man's legs, tripping him up.

17

Swearing loudly, Hack fell flat on his back with his legs in the air. How ridiculous he looks, thought Alfie.

Hack shook his fist and shouted, 'I'll get even with you one day, you'll see!'

'Hack!' shouted Fred from across the lines. 'This is no time to be lying down on the platform. Get on with your work!'

'It's that *cat*!' cried Hack, as he got to his feet. 'He's getting on my nerves. He's . . .'

Alfie didn't wait to hear any more. He decided there was just time to go to the front of the station to see if anything interesting was going on there, before meeting the local branch-line train, due in a few minutes.

## 2

# The Runaway Train

There was only one car parked on the station forecourt. The occupants were one young man who, Alfie guessed, was meeting someone off the next train from London – and two very large dogs. One of the dogs, with tongue hanging loose as he panted loudly, had thrust his head out of the open car window and was staring hard at Alfie.

Alfie bristled. Must keep well clear of those dogs, he thought. He turned to run back into the station when – being well used to train sounds – he heard an *unusual* noise. He glanced back, startled.

On time, the branch-line train was coming round the curve towards the station. Nothing wrong about that. *But* it was travelling far too fast. Whatever was happening? thought Alfie, very worried. It was freezing cold. Perhaps ice had formed on the lines and the train was skidding out of control?

Going at that speed, Alfie knew the train couldn't be halted before it crashed through the buffers right on to the station forecourt! And, apart from the train, what would happen to the car, which was right in the path of the train? And to the young man, who was reading a newspaper? And to the dogs?

Hardly realizing what he was doing, with the hair round his neck standing on end and his teeth bared, Alfie rushed at the car. Bravely, he sprang up at the car window and spat fiercely at the dogs.

Surprised, the young man looked up quickly as, barking fiercely, both dogs one after the other leapt out of the window and went after Alfie.

The young man's eyes widened in amazement and fright as he saw the yellow front of the branch train coming straight for him. He flung open the car door and jumped clear, just before the runaway train, with a grinding, crunching noise, smashed through the buffers and the barrier fence and careered into the parked car, crushing it into a tangled heap of metal.

Alfie had frantically clawed his way up a drainpipe and crouched down on the station roof. The dogs fled and the young man, in a dazed state, stumbled after them.

From his high vantage point, Alfie watched the scene below. All was confusion. The staff rushed out of the station. Fred ran back into the booking office and could be heard shouting at the top of his voice down the telephone.

20

'STATION URGENT. ACCIDENT!'

Peering over the guttering Alfie saw that the driver, still trapped in the engine cab, was waving his arms about and his lips were moving. So *he* can't be badly injured, thought Alfie, relieved. The passengers, unharmed but shaken, were being helped from the train.

Soon the police arrived, then a doctor and an ambulance. Alfie watched intently as the driver was lifted out of the cab. With a broken leg and a sore head, but managing to smile at his mates, he was driven off in the ambulance. Next, the passengers were seen off by Fred in a specially chartered bus.

21

At last, Fred stood back and mopped his brow. 'Phew! What a day!' he exclaimed. 'Thank goodness no one was seriously injured.' He glanced at the buckled train. 'There will be a lot of clearing up work to be done. The cranes will be along shortly to lift the train. Then we'll have to get rid of all the debris. And, of course, an inquiry will be held to find out the cause of the accident – ice on the track, I suspect.'

Fred looked at the car still underneath the train. 'I noticed a young man and two dogs in the car just before the accident,' he said, puzzled.

'Well, I caught sight of him running after the frightened dogs just before the crash,' said Hack. 'I've told the police.'

'Dogs,' said Fred. He had a sudden disturbing thought. 'Where's Alfie? Is *he* all right?'

Hearing his name, Alfie let out a piteous 'Miaow!' He had managed to scramble up the drainpipe, but he had no intention of risking his neck by sliding down it – especially with those dogs about!

'Ah, there you are, Alfie, safe and sound I hope,' cried Fred, with a sigh of relief. 'Fetch a ladder, Hack, and I'll bring him down.'

'Bothering about a cat,' said Hack as he went off.

'Sharp!' snapped Fred.

When Hack returned, Fred shinned up the ladder,

tucked Alfie under one arm and carried him down carefully.

'Always drawing attention to himself, that cat,' said Hack. 'Beats me why we have to put up with him.'

Fred turned to him. 'Listen to me, Hack, once and for all,' he cried. 'Alfie is the railway cat. He *belongs* here . . .'

He was interrupted by the young man running up with the dogs. (Alfie dug his claws into Fred's jacket!) 'I've found the dogs,' panted the young man. 'They were frightened out of their wits – so was I.'

His eyes rested on the crushed car, then he saw Alfie. 'My goodness!' he cried, 'if it hadn't been for that cat, the dogs and I would have been crushed under the train.'

'Cat? You mean Alfie?' said Fred.

'Yes, Alfie, if that's his name. Saved our lives. He rushed up and spat at the dogs. They jumped out of the car. I wouldn't have got out in time if Alfie hadn't disturbed me . . .' He shook his head at the thought and gazed at Alfie in admiration.

'All's well that ends well,' said Fred, beaming. 'Hear that, Hack? "Bothering about a cat," did I hear you say? Why, he's a hero, our Alfie! The reporters will be along soon. His picture will be in the newspapers. He might even appear on television.'

23

'Huh!' said Hack, scornfully. 'That cat on television? Whatever next. I can't abide cats – least of all Alfie.'

'Here they come!' cried Fred, as a television van drove up. The crew unloaded cameras and proceeded to film the damaged train, the car, the young man and the staff, including Alfie – especially Alfie!

And reporters from local and national newspapers came along with cameramen, and they took photographs of everything and everyone – especially of Alfie!

Very soon a crane arrived and the lifting process began. More pictures were taken – of Alfie sitting right on top of the crane – and of Alfie beside the mangled car.

'It's all that cat!' cried Hack, exasperated. 'You'd think no one else had done anything.'

Meanwhile, the young man and the dogs were taken home in a police car. (Alfie was thankful to see them go.) Things didn't settle down until late afternoon when Fred went home for a well-earned rest. When he returned in the evening he told Alfie, 'There were pictures of us all on television – and lots more of you than of anyone else, you clever cat. You're famous!'

Alfie just said, 'Miaow!' but for the rest of the evening stalked about with his head and tail held high.

Next morning, the commuters showed Alfie his photographs on front pages of the newspapers.

## THE CAT WHO SAVED THREE LIVES WHEN
## A TRAIN SKIDDED ON ICE

was printed underneath the pictures.

Actually, Alfie couldn't imagine what all the fuss was about.

'If *you* saw a car right in the path of a train, you'd try and do something, wouldn't you?' he wanted to ask everybody. There were times when he got very impatient with people for not understanding cat language. But Alfie purred all day. The only unhappy person on the station was Hack.

'That cat will be so conceited after all the fuss, there'll be no holding him,' he muttered from time to time.

But, of course, he didn't speak out loud, for Alfie was far too popular with everyone.

Passengers brought presents for Alfie, the hero – a nice morsel of fish perhaps, or a piece of crispy bacon. Soon he was in danger of becoming a fat cat and – it must be admitted – a lazy cat. For instance, one morning as he was squatting on the platform, two mice ran right in front of him almost brushing his whiskers. And he didn't give chase!

Oh, dear! Oh, dear! I can't go on like this, thought Alfie as he glanced guiltily over his shoulder to see if anyone else had noticed the mice.

Someone else had – Hack!

'That cat's getting bone idle!' said Hack to Fred who came up at that moment. 'He's just let two mice run almost across his nose. What he needs is a good prod.' He moved a foot in Alfie's direction.

'Don't dare touch him!' cried Fred. 'I've asked the passengers to stop feeding him. He'll be quite all right with less food and more exercise.'

Alfie moved his head from side to side as Fred rubbed the soft fur under his chin. He purred with pride when Fred added, 'He's the best railway cat we've ever had.'

It was not long before Alfie was his old active self. First, he cleared the station of several mice that had taken advantage of Alfie's laziness to invade the station. He took his duties seriously again and saw the arrival and departure of every train.

There was never a dull moment.

# 3

# Alfie is Marooned

It was getting much colder. One day Alfie shivered as he glanced up at the darkening sky. A passenger called out to him, 'It's going to snow soon – mind you keep warm, Alfie.'

Sure enough, next morning Alfie woke to find the station covered in dazzling white snow. He had to lift his paws high as he stepped hesitantly down the platform and over the bridge on his way to the staff room. He opened his mouth wide and let a large cold flake settle on his tongue.

Alfie thought it was great fun. Some children arrived at the station on sledges pulled by grown-ups. Alfie was given a ride up and down the station road. And he didn't object when, occasionally, he was accidentally hit by soft round snowballs, which flew into little pieces all over his fur.

For two weeks it snowed. In spite of Hack's sweeping, the platforms were always covered in dirty slush. Snow-ploughs were at work on the lines. Passengers looked weary because trains were delayed (the actor complained to Hack because he was late for rehearsals) and everybody shook and shivered in the cold.

Worst of all – so far as Alfie was concerned – Fred caught a severe chill and had to stay at home. And, as might be expected, one evening Alfie had no supper and no breakfast next morning. Hack took no notice of him.

Alfie decided to give Hack a sharp reminder of his duties. He waited until a two-coach diesel train, with few passengers aboard, came in. Then when Hack came along, he jumped up, stuck his claws into the man's jacket and hung on for all he was worth.

'Hey – what do you think you're doing?' cried Hack as he tried to shake him off. 'Can't attend to *you* yet.'

Alfie clung on for a time then fell back on to the platform. Hack looked round quickly. No one nearby. He picked Alfie up, thrust him into the train and slammed the door shut.

'That's got rid of you for the time being,' he yelled, as he put a hand to his head. (He looked slightly ashamed of himself!)

A whistle was sounded and the train moved away. Alfie felt bewildered. Although he was the railway cat, he'd never before travelled on a train. He walked down the gangway miaowing at the few people sitting on either side. They looked down, surprised.

'Why! It's Alfie!' cried old Granny Davies.

'What's he doing on the train?' said Farmer Cox.

The guard came along. He laughed when he saw Alfie. 'Come for the ride, have you, Alfie?' he said.

'Well, you'll be nice and warm in here with the passengers.'

'Shall we stop the train and send him back to the station?' someone asked.

'Oh, no, no, no,' said the guard. 'Alfie can travel with me to the terminus – *he* doesn't need a ticket! I'll see he gets back safely.'

'He's miaowing a lot,' said Granny Davies.

'Perhaps he's hungry,' said the farmer.

'Hmmm . . . might well be,' said the guard thoughtfully. 'Fred's away ill and Hack, well – *he's* got a lot on his mind at the moment. Probably hasn't bothered about Alfie. Fred will be furious.'

'Perhaps Alfie would like some tea from my flask,' said Granny Davies, who was sitting, well wrapped up, in the middle of the coach.

'That's a good idea,' said the guard. 'There's a bottle of milk in the van. I'll go and get it.'

He soon returned with the milk and a saucer. Alfie eagerly drank the warm tea and milk. Then another passenger produced a lunch packet. He carefully removed the cheese out of two large sandwiches and offered it to Alfie.

Now if there was one thing Alfie enjoyed almost as much as fish, it was cheese. It's my lucky day, he thought.

31

'Well, that's settled Alfie,' said the guard smiling. 'I'll tell the driver we've got a VIP on board.' He went forward to the driver's cab.

Alfie had a marvellous time. He felt quite skittish as he leapt over the backs of seats from one lap to another. His head jerked from side to side and his eyes opened wide in amazement as he gazed through the window at the snowy fields, with sheep and cattle huddled against fences and trees bending beneath the weight of snow. It was still snowing hard, a real blizzard.

'Hope we don't get snow-bound,' said Granny Davies nervously.

'Perhaps we shouldn't have left the station,' said a boy.

Just after they had passed over a canal, covered in glassy ice, Alfie noticed that the train was slowing down. Slower and slower it moved until at last it came to a halt. Right in the middle of nowhere, it seemed to Alfie – not a human being, nor a building in sight.

The driver jumped down to examine the track ahead. He returned shaking his head. 'The line's completely blocked by a massive snow-drift,' he announced. 'There's no chance of driving through *that*.'

'I'll have to walk back to the nearest line-side telephone . . .' said the guard promptly.

'Only a quarter of a mile away,' put in the driver.

The guard nodded. 'I'll phone the control office and report that we're stuck.'

'We'll have to sit it out until we're rescued,' the driver told the passengers. 'I'll keep the heating going. Can't risk Granny Davies getting a chill.'

'Do you think we'll have to spend the night here?' Granny Davies asked in a trembling voice.

'Very unlikely,' said the guard.

'Last winter we were marooned on our farm for twenty days,' said the farmer.

'Oh, dear!' sighed Granny Davies. (Alfie hoped the farmer had had enough food to last twenty days. *He* didn't think he'd be able to manage so long without food!)

They all cheered as the guard started to make his way carefully along the side of the line. The going was difficult for snow was already building up again over the track, which earlier in the day had been cleared by a snow-plough.

Alfie thought being marooned was great fun. Passengers from the other coach, and the driver joined them. Someone started singing and Alfie helped by miaowing occasionally. Everyone laughed and encouraged him to do it again.

It wasn't very long before the guard could be seen struggling back through the snow. 'I got through to control,' he reported. 'We must just sit tight and await developments.'

Alfie didn't mind. Everyone was so jolly that time passed very quickly. Suddenly the noise of the engine ceased.

'Hello, what's up?' cried the driver, as he made his way to the cab.

He returned after a time, looking worried. 'The heating's gone off because we have run out of fuel – never happened to me before,' he told them. He glanced at Granny Davies. 'We must keep Granny warm.'

He covered her with his own top coat. Someone produced a scarf, which was wound round her hat. Alfie thought she looked very funny.

But it got colder and colder. Granny Davies started complaining, 'It's my *feet*. Might just as well be in a refrigerator,' she said, her teeth chattering. 'If only my *feet* were warm, I'm sure the rest of me would be all right.' A cardigan was wrapped round her feet and for a time the old lady was quiet. Alfie had curled up on a seat beside the farmer, who was fat and comfortable. Alfie didn't mind the cold, but soon Granny Davies became more and more distressed.

'Just like blocks of ice, my feet,' she moaned.

The guard and driver looked at her in dismay. 'She's going blue in the face,' whispered the guard. 'It would be very serious, at her age, if she caught pneumonia.'

'What a pity we haven't got a hot-water bottle,' said the driver.

'What about Alfie?' said the farmer suddenly.

'Alfie?'

'Yes, Alfie. *He's* as warm as toast. Feel him.'

Everyone laughed as the guard unwound the cardigan from round Granny's feet – and put Alfie there instead!

'See if you can do the trick, old chap,' said the guard, smiling. 'Don't worry, Granny, I'm sure Alfie will keep you warm.'

And he did!

Colour came back into the old lady's cheeks and she

beamed at everyone. 'Alfie's much better than a hot-water bottle,' she said. 'He's as good as a warm fur muff!'

Time passed and Alfie stayed quietly on Granny's feet. He dozed off now and then as he half-listened to the murmur of voices round him. He woke up suddenly when everyone stopped talking. A throbbing, whirring noise, which Alfie didn't recognize, could be heard. Could it be a train with snow-plough attached coming to the rescue? Or an aeroplane? The passengers were staring out of the windows and soon Alfie heard them all shouting at once,

'Why, it's a helicopter!'

'Coming to our rescue.'

Alfie leapt off Granny's feet and on to a seat. With his paws on a window ledge he watched the helicopter as it hovered over a field just beyond the railway embankment.

'What a good thing there are no high tension cables near here,' said the guard. 'The helicopter will be able to make a perfect landing.'

As the machine touched ground everyone in the train waved and cheered and Alfie miaowed as loudly as possible. And, in no time at all, it seemed to Alfie, they were all, a few at a time, taken aboard the helicopter and ferried to the airfield a few miles away.

Alfie, with the guard and driver, was last to leave. What a day it had been, he thought. His first train journey, and now a helicopter flight. His only regret was that he hadn't been winched aboard – that would have been very exciting!

He felt dizzy as, held by the guard, he gazed below at the canal and fields. After about ten minutes, he craned his neck to see what looked like his own station far below. But they were passing right over it! Was he ever going to get home?

They landed on the airfield and after a car journey with the guard and driver, Alfie found himself back at his own station. And, in spite of all the adventures, he was pleased to be back. For how could the station be properly managed without the assistance of the railway cat?

'Magnificent cat, Alfie,' the guard said to Hack. 'I'm sure he saved Granny Davies's life.' He stared hard at Hack. *'Don't forget to feed him,'* he added.

Hack snorted. Nevertheless, he led the way to the staff room and fed Alfie. 'You'd better stay in here for the night, it's warmer than the waiting room,' he said gruffly. 'I'll leave the radiator on for you.'

He turned at the door. 'Expect your picture will be in the newspapers again,' he said, as he slammed the door and locked it behind him.

Ah, well, thought Alfie as he curled up in the only comfortable chair, perhaps Hack's bark is worse than his bite.

Next morning, Alfie's picture was in the newspapers.

## THE SNOW-BOUND CAT WHO SAVED AN OLD LADY'S LIFE

said the caption. That was an exaggeration, thought Alfie – but it had all been great fun. I'll go for another train trip one day, he promised himself.

## 4

# Hack Has a Fright

Alfie was happy. Fred was back at work. The snow had gone and it was getting near to Christmas. He knew that no trains would run on Christmas Day, so the station would be closed. But he wasn't worried about that.

For as long as he could remember, Fred had come to the station twice on Christmas Day. Each time he had brought with him a dish of turkey. Alfie's mouth watered at the very thought of that tender meat.

Everyone was very cheerful. Even Hack was seen to smile – once! But Alfie was careful to keep out of the man's way. Christmas was a time of goodwill, and he didn't want to upset Hack again.

One day a group of students dashed off a train as soon as it pulled up at the bay platform. In high spirits they laughed and joked as they made their way to the exit. They stopped to offer a sweet to Alfie. He took it carefully between his teeth before chewing and swallowing it. Not bad, he thought, but he hoped the students didn't think sweets were his favourite food.

(Just think of Fred's turkey!) Still, it was kind of the boys.

Fred appeared. He smiled at the students. 'Don't give Alfie too many sweets. He'll be getting fat again,' he said.

Several students spoke at the same time.

'Oh, no, no, no – we won't do that.'

'We'd . . . er . . . better be going.'

'Yes, let's scram!'

They seemed very excited as, laughing and jostling one another, they went through the exit and ran down the road.

Fred stroked his chin. 'Hmmm . . .' he said, 'I wonder why they are in such a hurry?'

Alfie decided to stroll across to the bay platform to find out if a crisp or two, or a sweet had been left behind in the train. He knew that the train, its doors wide open, standing at the platform wasn't due out for another twenty minutes.

He jumped in and started to search the first coach by leaping on to all the seats and then crawling underneath them. But, apart from a couple of newspapers and a sweet paper with not a trace of sticky sugar left on it, Alfie drew a blank.

He'd just emerged from under the last seat when – what was that? He froze in horror – his fur stood on end

and he felt as prickly as a porcupine. With one paw in the air, and tail quivering, he stared at a great hairy monster, with massive shoulders and staring eyes, which was slumped between two seats.

Alfie stood rigid for at least half a minute. He was about to turn and rush out of the train in terror, when he noticed something which made him stop. The beast's eyes in its black and wrinkled face didn't flicker and its long arms hung limply.

Was the monster ill? Overcoming his fright, Alfie crept forward on his stomach. He put out a paw and touched the beast's leg, before springing back warily – but the animal didn't move. Alfie waited a moment, then he went nearer and looked into the marble-like eyes.

Then Alfie understood – the thing was *stuffed*. Now what on earth was a strange thing like a stuffed animal doing in a train at Alfie's station? He knew that cheque books, credit cards and pocket calculators – and umbrellas! – among other things, were often left in trains, but this beat everything!

Just then Alfie heard Hack shouting to someone as he approached the bay platform. Goodness, I don't think Hack's very brave. He's going to get the shock of his life (and be more bad-tempered than ever) if he comes on this monster unawares. Alfie was worried.

How could he warn Hack? He thought for a moment, then he crept, out of sight, under the animal's slightly raised left arm. As Hack came abreast of the train, Alfie filled his lungs before letting out a hideous howling noise. He felt quite proud of his efforts, so he did it again – and again. That should warn Hack, who would probably go running for Fred, and nothing ever scared Fred.

However, startled but curious, Hack stepped cautiously into the train and made his way slowly down the coach, searching the seats, the luggage racks and, occasionally, bending down to glance under the seats.

Just before Hack sighted the monster, Alfie howled again. (Better than before, he thought!) Shocked and unable to believe his eyes or his ears, Hack halted. Rooted to the spot, he gazed and gazed at the beast confronting him. Alfie, still out of sight, moved and the animal appeared to raise its arm slightly.

This was too much for Hack. Shrieking 'Ahh . . . ahhhaaa . . . aaa . . . aaa . . . !' he rushed down the gangway, leapt out of the train – and bumped right into Fred.

'Hey there, look where you're going!' cried Fred. 'Whatever's the matter?'

Hack gulped. He had difficulty in speaking. 'It . . . it . . . it's in . . . in *there*.' He gulped again and waved a shaking arm towards the train.

'*What's* in there?' asked Fred, irritated.

'A . . . a terr . . . if . . . ific thing, a mon . . . mon . . . *monster* – a great, staring, hairy, mon . . . mon . . . monster!'

'Don't be silly – you've been dreaming!' cried Fred, as he took hold of Hack by the shoulders and shook him.

At this moment Alfie howled again. (He was quite enjoying himself.)

'Listen – that's it!' gasped Hack. He turned to flee, but Fred clutched his arm and held him back.

'No running away. We're on duty – remember,' he said sternly. 'Come on, show me the monster.'

Still holding on to Hack, he boarded the train. By now, Brown and several other people had arrived to find out what all the noise was about. They all trooped into the train.

Fred's eyes widened and he gasped in surprise when he saw the monster. He drew back hastily. Then, squaring his shoulders, he leaned forward and peered at the beast. He burst out laughing as he caught sight of two round green eyes staring at him from underneath the monster's hairy arm.

'Thought so!' he cried. 'Come out, Alfie. Let Hack take a look at you.'

Obligingly Alfie jumped clear and the beast's arm fell back into position.

'You're right, Hack,' cried Fred, choking with mirth, 'it is a monster – of sorts. It's a stuffed *gorilla*!'

Everyone, except Hack, thought it was hilarious, but Hack shuffled his feet and scowled at Alfie.

'Oh, dear! Oh, dear! I feel helpless with laughing,' cried Fred, as he clung to the back of a seat. 'Who would have thought our Alfie could make a noise which would frighten Hack nearly out of his wits?'

Hack was very put out. 'That cat's always trying to take the mickey out of me,' he shouted. 'I shan't forget this in a hurry.'

'Now, now, calm down, Hack,' said Fred. 'No harm's been done and I'm sure Alfie was only trying to be helpful.'

Hack shouted, 'Helpful? Him? He's as helpful as a cartload of monkeys.'

'What I'm wondering,' put in Brown, 'is how did the gorilla get into the train?'

Fred had an answer. 'Remember the students coming off the train earlier on? Well, I wondered why they made off in such a hurry. My guess is that they stole the gorilla from a museum – or from a private collection, perhaps – just for a lark. Then they didn't know what to do with it, so left it on the train.'

'Well, I must say it was very clever of them to get it out of a museum without being detected, and then on to a train without anyone noticing,' said Brown.

Fred nodded. 'There'll be a row about this,' he said. 'Railway staff and museum staff will have to be more on the alert in future. Still – it's getting near to Christmas and I suppose students, like most people, are feeling light-hearted . . .'

In the event, the students got a good ticking off from various quarters and promised never to do such a thing again. But Alfie thought that, if he knew anything about students, it wouldn't be long before they got up to more mischief. He must practise making hideous noises in case they came in useful!

Everyone, except Hack, liked talking about the gorilla. But Hack walked about with a frown on his face, which deepened whenever he caught sight of Alfie.

Alfie sighed. After all, he'd only tried to save Hack from getting a shock. But, he had to admit, he *had* enjoyed making those wonderful gorilla noises . . .

# 5

# A Trip to London

It was only ten days to Christmas. Alfie watched mothers going by train to a nearby town and returning laden with Christmas shopping. He listened to children talking excitedly about school plays, parties and presents. He could hardly wait for Christmas.

'Looking forward to the turkey, Alfie?' Fred would ask jokingly.

Only Hack went about with never a smile on his face. One morning when Alfie was standing by the actor, who was waiting for a London train, Hack came up suddenly. (Alfie decided that it would be undignified to dash off, so he stayed where he was and listened. In any case, Alfie was still waiting for his breakfast.)

'Good morning, Hack,' said the actor pleasantly, as he breathed in deeply. 'It's a nice, crisp day, isn't it?' He stared at Hack. 'I wonder why you always look so, well, er . . . sort of glum?'

Hack muttered something under his breath, then he turned and saw Alfie. '. . . and that cat, always getting in the way, always wanting food,' (not true, thought

Alfie) 'always showing off,' (Really!) 'and I haven't forgotten how he made a fool of me with his imitation gorilla noises.' (And very good noises they were, said Alfie to himself.)

The actor gazed at Alfie as if he'd never seen him before. 'He's a fine, handsome, beautifully marked cat . . .' he said, thoughtfully.

'Miaow!' said Alfie, very pleased that Hack was listening.

'. . . I wonder? Hack! I've just had a marvellous idea. The pantomime is due to start tomorrow night – and we're in a right fix. We could do with a live cat. I think

50

Alfie would solve the problem. I'll take him with me if you like.'

'Take him? Will you, really?' said Hack eagerly. He looked round guiltily to make sure Fred wasn't in sight. 'But he hasn't been fed yet.'

'All the better for that,' said the actor. He held out a canvas bag. 'Quick! Slip him in here. No one's taking any notice. They're all reading the morning papers.'

Before Alfie had time to realize what was happening, Hack swooped down, picked him up and popped him into the bag. The train came in and Alfie wailed loudly as he was carried into a compartment. He struggled and scratched the inside of the bag when he felt the train move off.

Alfie had never been shut up like this before, and he complained bitterly at the loss of his self-respect. He was very worried. Whatever had the actor meant when he had said it was all the better that Alfie hadn't been fed? And what did he want with a cat – a *live* cat – anyhow? Alfie moaned loudly as he kicked and scratched again.

'What have you got in there?' he heard a man ask.

'Oh, it's only my son's cat. I'm taking him to London for a check-up.'

What lies, thought poor Alfie. To add to his miseries he began to feel he was suffocating, and was very relieved when the bag was opened about an inch. He tried with all his strength to claw his way out.

But the actor patted the bag reassuringly. 'Keep quiet, Alfie,' he whispered. 'We'll soon be in London.'

At the third stop the actor (and Alfie) left the train. Alfie guessed by the noise and bustle – much much louder than at his own station – that they must be at the London railway terminus. He'd always wanted to visit London, but he might just as well have been in a small stuffy cave for all he could see.

The actor hailed a taxi. 'To the Dolphin Theatre,' he said. He jumped in and carefully put the bag beside him on the seat.

'Nearly there, Alfie,' he said.

The bag, with Alfie inside, swayed as the driver swerved and braked in the traffic. Alfie didn't think he'd have much chance of finding his way home through the London traffic, even if he managed to escape from the actor.

Soon they arrived at the theatre.

'The producer wants to see you urgently, sir,' said the doorkeeper as they entered the building through the stage door. 'He's got the jitters,' he added.

'I'll cure his jitters,' said the actor smiling. He went down a passage towards the stage.

'Oh, thank goodness you've arrived!' exclaimed the

producer. 'We're in real trouble. The "cat" man is still off ill and, worse still, we can't find a replacement anywhere. We've tried the agencies, but all suitable actors are booked for the Christmas season. We can't possibly do the show without a *cat*.'

'He's in here,' said the actor, laughing.

'*Who's* in *where*?' said the producer, puzzled.

'Alfie. In the bag. I suggest we use a real live cat instead of a man dressed up as a cat. The children will love Alfie, and I'm sure we'll be able to train him at rehearsal tonight in time for the opening tomorrow.'

'Phew!' said the producer, wiping his forehead. 'I hope you're right. Let's have a look at him.'

'Come along to my dressing room. Can't risk him escaping,' said the actor.

Thankfully Alfie jumped out of the bag as soon as it was opened. He found himself in a small room. The first thing he noticed was a large mirror over a wide dressing table. On the table were jars, tubes and brushes. Hung on hooks round the walls were fancy costumes and hats. Several pairs of boots and shoes were on the floor.

'Well, what do you think of Alfie?' asked the actor.

'He's certainly a fine-looking animal,' was the reply, 'but do you *really* think he'll be able to play the part?'

'Certainly he will – with a little "fishy" help, of course!' laughed the actor.

'Well . . . we'll see,' said the producer doubtfully. 'In any case, he's our only hope. You'd better get dressed. I'll call a rehearsal to begin in an hour's time.'

'I'll be ready,' said the actor. 'Will you send someone for milk and fish for *after* the show, and a basket?'

After the producer had left, the actor said, 'I'm relying on you to do your best, Alfie.'

Now Alfie always believed in doing his best in everything, but what was he supposed to be doing his best for in this case?

'First, you'll have some milk,' the actor went on, 'and, later on, some fish. What more could you want?'

'Miaow! Miaow! Miaow!' wailed Alfie, which meant, 'I want to go straight back to my railway station.'

However, being a sensible cat, as well as a clever one, he decided there was nothing he could do for the time being, but obey orders.

There was a knock on the door and a man entered with a bottle of milk, a paper-wrapped parcel of fish (Alfie could smell it!) and a wide, flat basket.

'Here you are, Alfie,' said the actor, as he poured some milk into a saucer and put it on the floor in front of Alfie. When Alfie had finished lapping up the milk, he said, 'Miaow!' which meant, 'I'm ready for the fish now.'

But he wasn't given any fish! The parcel had been

55

placed on a high shelf so, with his eyes, Alfie measured the distance from floor to a chair, and then from chair to shelf. He got ready to spring, but the actor put out a hand.

'It's not time for the fish yet, Alfie,' he said. 'You'll have to be patient until *after the show*.'

After the show? What did that mean, thought Alfie. Why, he hadn't had a bite to eat since Fred had given him his supper last evening! The thought of Fred – and of the turkey he might never taste – made Alfie feel very sad. He miaowed quietly.

'Oh, don't worry, everything will be all right, Alfie,' said the actor, kindly. 'Just do as I tell you and you'll get your fish eventually.'

The man started to dress for the show, in ragged clothes. Then he made a few more rags into a bundle, which he tied to the end of a stick. He was barefooted and looked like a poor waif. Alfie was puzzled, until the actor explained.

'Listen carefully, Alfie. In the pantomime, *I'm* Dick Whittington and *you're* my cat.' He stretched up and took the parcel of fish from the shelf. 'You're going to follow this fish about the stage. If I'm holding it, you follow me. If another actor has it, you follow him. Understand?'

'Miaow!' said Alfie. He didn't really understand why

he couldn't have the fish before the show, but he was ready to do his best and the thought of supper spurred him on.

The actor bent down and fastened a collar and lead round Alfie's neck. Alfie was outraged. He struggled wildly and made angry noises.

'Now, now, that's enough,' cried the actor. 'It's only for the rehearsal. I'm sure you'll be able to act without the collar and lead in the real performance.'

He led Alfie out of the room and down a corridor towards the back of the stage. The lights were dazzling and the noise almost deafening. There were so many people standing about, some in costume and others in ordinary working clothes, that Alfie felt quite bewildered.

But everyone seemed pleased to see Alfie, and to admire him.

'He's a very handsome cat.'

'Quite a character, I should imagine.'

'Best of luck, Alfie. Don't let us down.'

'He won't let us down. He'll steal the show if we're not careful!'

And – to start with – Alfie *did* steal the rehearsal.

# 6

# Alfie Follows the Fish

From the moment it was Alfie's turn to go on stage he was a sensation. With head held high he stepped proudly after Dick Whittington (and the fish!) without having to be pulled. He looked round with interest, and when the chorus started singing, Alfie opened his mouth, threw back his head and joined in,

'Miao . . . aow . . . aow . . . iaow!'

Everybody laughed so much that the rehearsal had to stop. The producer, wiping tears of mirth from his eyes, called out,

'Go on! Go on! Let him join in – the children will love it tomorrow.'

There was only one thing which bothered Alfie at first, and that was a man dressed in black with a white shirt, who was standing just beyond the footlights with his back to the audience. Alfie couldn't understand why the man kept waving a little white stick at him.

Alfie didn't approve of sticks being waved at anyone! So the first time he got close enough to the footlights, he craned his neck and hissed loudly at the conductor of

the orchestra. He even – although he knew it wasn't good manners – spat at him once! To Alfie's surprise, everyone burst out laughing again and the rehearsal came to a halt.

'Oh, do get on with it, please,' implored the producer. 'It's fine – just fine. Alfie will have the children jumping about with excitement.'

So the rehearsal continued, and Alfie began to understand what the play was about. It appeared that Dick Whittington, the ragged hungry waif, who had come to London to seek his fortune, didn't find the London streets paved with gold as he had been led to believe. Instead, he had to work for a cook who scolded and beat him all the time. He was made to sleep in an attic overrun with rats and mice.

And that was where Alfie came in. Dick bought him in a market for *one penny*. (What an insult, thought Alfie. He was glad Hack wasn't about – still, it was only a story.)

Alfie followed Dick (and the fish!) about the stage. He got rid of all the rats and mice in Dick's attic bedroom. To his disgust, they were battery-operated rats and mice!

Dick badly needed money, so he gave Alfie to a sea captain to sell for him. But Dick was so unhappy because he had sent his cat away, that he decided to run

away himself. But the bells of Bow Church rang out and
seemed to be singing,

> 'Turn again, Whittington,
> Lord Mayor of London,
> Turn again, Whittington,
> Thrice Mayor of London.'

so Dick turned back.

Meanwhile, Alfie followed the sea captain (and the
fish!) and soon cleared the ship of hundreds of rats and
mice. When they arrived at a far country, they found
the king's palace overrun with rats and mice too. (What
a lot of rats and mice there were in this pantomime
world, thought Alfie. If only they were *real*!) Anyway,
Alfie chased them all out of the kingdom.

The king was so pleased with Alfie that he gave the
sea captain a *casket full of gold and jewels* to take back to
Dick Whittington in payment for his cat. (Alfie
wouldn't have minded Hack hearing about this.) So
Alfie stayed in the far country and followed the king
(and the fish!) while the sea captain sailed back to
London with the casket.

The gold and jewels made Dick Whittington a very
rich man and, as Bow Bells had foretold, he became
Lord Mayor of London, not once, but three times. And
all because of his cat – that's *me*, thought Alfie. He was

very pleased that everything had turned out so well, even if it was only make-believe.

The producer and the cast were all full of praise for Alfie and all agreed he was the star of the show.

'He can't put a paw wrong,' said the producer.

Alfie was glad he'd given satisfaction, but he was getting hungrier and hungrier. Eventually he followed the actor (and the fish!) back to the dressing room, and at last – at long last! – the railway cat had his supper.

Later on he settled down in the basket. The actor told him, 'I'm going home now, Alfie. You'll be quite comfortable here. The night watchman will look in on you during the night.' Off he went.

Alfie knew the actor would be travelling by train to Alfie's own railway station, where Fred would be on duty to meet the late night train. How Alfie longed to see Fred again. He wouldn't mind even seeing Hack as well.

For the next few days – every evening (except Sunday) and two matinees – Alfie took part in the pantomime – without the collar and lead. He had no food until after the evening shows. He was definitely a hit. The children loved him and cheered and clapped whenever he appeared. The show played to packed houses as news of Alfie's success spread.

Alfie enjoyed it at first, but gradually he became restless. This was no job for a railway cat. His thoughts

turned more and more to his real life on the station – the staff, passengers, happy children, and Granny Davies on her way to visit her daughter for Christmas. Sadly, Alfie hoped they were all missing him.

One afternoon – just two days before Christmas – Alfie followed the fish on to the stage as usual. There were hundreds of children in the audience and they gave Alfie a rapturous reception. This particular afternoon, after the applause had died down, he heard a shrill voice in the audience calling out,

'But it *is* Alfie. I'm sure it is!'

'Ssh! Ssh! Ssh!' came from all sides.

'*But it is . . .*'

'Quiet, please,' shouted someone, and the shrill young voice was heard no more. Apparently no one on stage, except Alfie, had heard.

Alfie had difficulty in concentrating on his part in the show. Had someone really recognized him? Was he going to be rescued? Afterwards, resting in the dressing room between shows, he was excited – and hopeful. Unable to settle down, he got up and started to prowl round the room.

'What's the matter, Alfie?' asked the actor, who had been reading a newspaper. 'I hope you're not sickening for something. That would be a pity after your success in the show.'

'Miaow!' said Alfie. He didn't care about success. Only about getting back to his station.

During the evening show he went as near to the footlights as he dared, in case anyone recognized him again. But no one shouted, 'It *is* Alfie!' and his spirits sank.

Back in the dressing room he ate his supper without any real enjoyment. He ate to keep up his strength, for he was determined that if he wasn't rescued very soon, he would try to escape . . . .

But suddenly there was a peremptory knock, the door burst open and in walked – Fred! Alfie stared for a moment, unable to believe his eyes. Then he made a mad rush. Fred picked him up and hugged him hard. Alfie purred and purred and purred – and *purred*. He'd never felt so relieved and happy in all his life.

'My word, Alfie, it is *good* to see you,' sighed Fred. 'Young Ted Asprey told me he was certain he'd seen you in the show. I caught the very next train. I hear you've been a terrific success but . . .' He turned to the actor, who sat in a chair, with make-up still on his face.

'As for *you*,' shouted Fred. 'Listen. Alfie is not a pantomime cat, and never will be. He's our *railway cat*. Don't ever forget that again, or I'll . . . I'll . . . I'll have the *law* on you.'

The actor looked very crestfallen. 'I'm sorry – I didn't stop to think . . .'

'Well, you should think!' cried Fred, scornfully.

'But we were in such trouble because we couldn't find anyone to play the cat. I thought it was a brilliant idea to have Alfie. He could earn thousands of pounds as a stage cat,' said the actor.

'Miaow!' growled Alfie, and hissed.

'He's *not a stage cat*,' roared Fred. 'You'd better watch out, or else . . .'

The actor shrank back in his chair. 'All right, all right,' he said hastily. 'I've said I'm sorry and you can see for yourself that Alfie has come to no harm.'

He sighed heavily. 'I really don't know what we're going to do without him. I'm afraid the show will have to close and we'll all be out of a job.'

'That's your problem,' said Fred.

Alfie was beginning to feel just a bit sorry for the man (after all he had been kind), and for the rest of the cast, when there was a rap on the door and in walked the producer.

He looked from one to the other. 'What's the matter?' he asked.

'We're in trouble again,' sighed the actor. 'Fred insists on taking Alfie back with him.'

'Alfie is our railway cat, and you had no right to take him away,' said Fred, his voice trembling with indignation.

The producer turned to the actor. 'You didn't tell me Alfie came here without the owner's permission,' he said.

'I thought no one would mind,' said the actor miserably, 'and now Alfie's going, we'll all be out of work.'

'Well, as a matter of fact we won't,' said the producer. 'The actor who was originally cast as the cat is better. He's reporting for duty tomorrow, so we don't really need Alfie.'

Alfie felt very pleased about this but Fred shouted, 'That doesn't alter the fact that Alfie was, well – catnapped as you might say.'

'No, it doesn't,' agreed the producer, 'and you must be compensated. I cannot afford to pay gold and jewels for his services.' He grinned. 'But will one hundred pounds settle the matter?'

'One hundred pounds?' cried Fred. 'That's too . . . no, no, no it isn't too much. Alfie's worth every penny – and more. The money will go to the Railway Benevolent Fund. Suit you, Alfie?'

'Miaow!' said Alfie, pushing his head under Fred's chin.

'So that's settled,' said the producer, 'but we'll never have another actor like Alfie. It was a great experience working with him.'

'It really was,' agreed the actor. He looked at his watch. 'Goodness! I didn't realize it was so late,' he said. 'I won't be able to remove my make-up in time to catch the last train, so I'll stay here for the night. You'd better hurry, Fred.'

Fred nodded. 'Coming, Alfie?' he said.

Coming? Of course he was coming. Alfie wouldn't let Fred go home without him for all the fish in the sea!

# 7

# The Turkey – and More

The producer ordered a taxi, and Alfie left the theatre clinging to Fred's shoulder. He had no intention of removing his claws from Fred's jacket until he reached his own station. They caught the train just in time.

'Nothing but the best for Alfie,' said the guard as, with a flourish, he opened the door of a first-class compartment and ushered them in.

Fred talked to Alfie. The passengers talked to him. And Alfie purred all the way home. And – what a surprise! – late as it was, news of Alfie's homecoming had gone round the village. It seemed to him that half the population had turned out to welcome him. Brown came on his bicycle, but there was no sign of Hack.

Several children had been allowed to stay up. They pushed and struggled to take turns at stroking Alfie. Suddenly he heard a voice among all the hubbub of conversation.

'*I* saw you first, in the theatre this afternoon, Alfie. *I* told Fred you were there,' and a small boy pushed his way to the front.

Alfie stretched out his front legs and then rolled over and over. 'Miaow! Miaow! Miaow!' he cried, by way of thanks.

It was well after midnight before everyone, except Fred, went home. Fred stayed behind to give Alfie a saucer of milk, and to settle him in his basket in the waiting room.

'You wouldn't believe how much we've missed you – even Hack, I think!' he said. 'But *I'll* make sure you get your breakfast tomorrow.' He bent down to stroke Alfie. 'Good night, Alfie. Sleep well.'

Alfie promptly fell asleep. He dreamt he heard bells (Bow Bells?) and imagined he saw a casket full of gold and silver and jewels, otherwise his sleep was undisturbed. He didn't wake up until the early-morning freight train chugged through the station.

He lost no time in making his way to the staff room to wait for Fred, but – surprise! surprise! – Hack's first duty was to feed Alfie. More surprising still, he even smiled – a lopsided sort of smile, but a smile neverthe-less.

Alfie could hardly believe it – had Hack turned over a new leaf, or was he afraid of being found out about his part in Alfie's disappearance?

After his meal, Alfie cleaned his fur, spruced his whiskers and prepared to greet the commuters, the

children, the shoppers . . . He sighed contentedly. Really, life at his own station on Christmas Eve was very satisfying.

The station was busy all day. Nearly everybody cried 'Merry Christmas!' and sometimes, 'Merry Christmas, Alfie – so glad you're back. The station wouldn't be the same without you.'

At last it was time for the station to be closed, the lights to be extinguished and for Fred to go home. Alfie went to bed. There was no early-morning train to wake him up on Christmas morning, so he had an extra lie-in.

When he did wake up, his first duty was to patrol the station twice, to make sure everything was in order. He knew Fred would be arriving soon with his breakfast turkey, and he could hardly contain his excitement.

To while away the waiting time, he frisked and frolicked along the platform, over the bridge and back again, chasing imaginary rats and mice. Suddenly, his sharp ears caught the sound of a key being turned stealthily in the entrance gate lock. That wasn't Fred! Fred always opened the door noisily, especially on Christmas mornings, and shouted,

'Alfie! You there, Alfie?'

Alfie crouched underneath the steps leading to the bridge. Up the other steps on the opposite platform crept a tall figure dressed in a red cloak and a red and white cap with a tassel on it. He had a long snowy-white beard and was carrying a sack over one shoulder.

Red cloak, white beard, sack – it must be a man dressed up as Father Christmas. How jolly, thought Alfie. He started to rush forward to meet this un-expected but welcome figure, when he stopped as a thought struck him.

Why was the man visiting the station on Christmas *Day* instead of Christmas *Eve*? Alfie sat down again, and waited. He watched the man walk over the bridge and down the steps. As he drew nearer, Alfie noticed that the man wore a mask. His eyes, through the slits, glanced furtively this way and that. Someone up to no good, thought Alfie. Now what . . . ?

The answer came to him suddenly. The man must be a burglar! He'd probably gone to an all-night party disguised as Father Christmas, and had come away with the loot – gold, jewels and silver ornaments, probably. Something heavy inside the sack clanked now and then as the man approached Alfie's hiding place.

Alfie was certain the burglar intended hiding th sack somewhere on the station. Then, next morning, he would come along with an empty suitcase, pick up the goods and catch the first fast train to London. What a very good detective I would make, thought Alfie.

He tensed his muscles, clenched his paws and sprang.

Taken by surprise, the man lost his balance and crashed heavily on to the platform. The sack caught him a sharp blow on the side of the head as he fell.

Muffled groans and screams could be heard coming from behind the mask as the man struggled to shake Alfie off his back. But Alfie had no intention of releasing him until Fred arrived. Every time the man tried to get to his feet, Alfie snarled, hissed, unsheathed his claws and threatened to bite and scratch.

Alfie hoped Fred would hurry up as he couldn't keep this up much longer. Soon, to his relief, he heard the gate opening and the familiar voice calling.

'Alfie! You there, Alfie?'

'*Miaow! Miaow! Miaow!*' howled Alfie.

Carrying a foil-covered dish in one hand, Fred rushed over the bridge and down the steps. He stared in amazement at the figure lying on the platform.

'Whatever's going on?' he wanted to know. 'What *are* you doing to Father Christmas, Alfie?'

But, to Alfie's surprise, Fred was laughing. 'Get up, Father Christmas,' he ordered. 'I'd recognize those eyes anywhere!'

Slowly the man rose to his feet.

'Now you'd better unmask,' said Fred, with a grin.

'No, no . . . I'll be getting off home,' muttered the man.

'Oh, no, you won't. Take it off, or shall I do it for you?' cried Fred.

'Oh, all right, all right,' said the man irritably.

Off came the mask and there stood – Hack! Alfie was so amazed that he couldn't even miaow.

Hack was very annoyed. 'That cat . . .' he began.

'Now, now, don't forget it's Christmas Day, a time for tolerance and goodwill,' Fred reminded him. 'But do tell Alfie and me *why* you've come to the station on Christmas Day dressed up as Father Christmas?'

Hack looked at the ground and shuffled his feet. Then he burst out, 'Well, if you want to know the truth, I'm tired of that cat giving me fright after fright *and* making a fool of me. I thought, just for a change, I'd turn the tables on him, creep up and scare the daylight out of him. Only a joke really. There was no need for him to attack me . . .'

'Alfie only *pretended* to attack you. He probably thought you were a trespasser or a burglar and it was up to him to do his duty.'

'Miaow!' said Alfie.

'I think it's time you two called a truce – at least for Christmas,' Fred went on.

'Miaow!' said Alfie again.

'I suppose so,' said Hack, grudgingly.

'That's settled then,' said Fred, beaming. 'And it's

high time Alfie had his Christmas breakfast.' He started to take the foil off the dish.

'Just a minute,' said Hack.

He picked up the sack, turned it upside down, shook it, and out fell – not gold or jewels or precious stones –

but four tins of cat food and two tins of lobster soup!

'Christmas present for Alfie,' said Hack, with a sidelong grin at Fred.

'Well, well, well, what do you think about that, Alfie?' said Fred. 'Aren't you a lucky cat?'

Alfie looked up at Hack, then he rolled over and over on his back, with his paws tucked up and his head back. Fred laughed out loud and Hack, well . . . he *almost* smiled.

Fred ripped off the foil. 'Turkey for Alfie now,' he said. 'You can start on the tinned food tomorrow.'

Alfie set to and – my goodness! – the turkey was as good, if not better than ever. Meanwhile, Hack picked up the tins and put them back into the sack. 'I'll bring them along tomorrow,' he promised. Fred and Hack waited until he had finished, then Alfie accompanied them as far as the gate. (He was the only one on duty today, he thought, proudly.)

'See you later, Alfie,' said Fred. He waved his hand. Alfie saw him nudge Hack, who rather reluctantly lifted an arm slightly, as if he *might* manage a wave, if he tried very hard.

Alfie laughed to himself. It was a very pleasant and unexpected feeling to have a wave from Hack on Christmas Day, even if it was only half a wave!

Alfie thought about the truce. Perhaps Hack had got used to him, even liked him – a little – or . . . but, never mind, he wouldn't bother about Hack until after Christmas.

Instead, he'd think of Fred (and the turkey) and about his duties as the railway cat.

# The Railway Cat
## and Digby

# Contents

# 1

# Station Visitors

A pale early morning sun shone through the waiting-room window. In his basket Alfie, the railway cat, stretched himself happily. Winter was nearly over. Spring days were ahead and there was plenty of activity at the station.

Today, for instance, Alfie's great friend Fred, the Chargeman, was going to show a group of school children round the station – and who better than Alfie to lead the way?

The railway cat left his basket and leapt through a partly-open ventilator on to the platform. He made his way over the bridge and sat down outside the staff-room door. Leading Railman Hack, who lived just up the road from the station, would be reporting for duty soon.

Not that Alfie especially wanted to see Hack, who was often grumpy, and didn't like cats – Alfie was ready for breakfast. He never minded seeing Hack's dog, Digby. As a matter of fact, although there was always a skirmish – just for fun – whenever the two animals met, Alfie really liked Digby. Alfie also got on well with

Hack's pigeons, occasionally chasing them off the station platform for a game.

But – hello, hello – what was this? Alfie blinked. Was he dreaming, or was Hack coming briskly towards him, calling out cheerfully, 'Sorry to keep you waiting, Alfie. I'll get your breakfast in two shakes of a lamb's tail.'

Alfie followed the man into the staff room. Sure enough, in about *ten* shakes of a lamb's tail (according to Alfie's reckoning) Hack placed a saucer of cat food and another saucer of milk on the floor. Alfie bent his head and set to. Breakfast was breakfast whoever served it.

As he lapped the milk he wondered why Hack was so happy and excited this morning. Then he remembered. Of course – Punch! Hack's racing pigeon Punch, had been entered in a national long-distance race. The bird was expected to return to Hack's garden loft some time this morning, to be timed in. Punch had been tipped favourite to win the race.

Alfie raised his head as Hack spoke. 'Fred's given me permission to go off duty for an hour or so after the rush period. I must be near my pigeon loft to check Punch's arrival time. Very important race this, Alfie.'

'Miaow!' agreed Alfie, as he put his head down again.

When he had finished his meal, Alfie strolled over to

the main exit. While he waited for Fred to arrive, he sat down and started to wash himself. He gave his long shiny whiskers and eyebrows special attention.

Fred came along. 'Good morning, Alfie,' he cried. 'Getting ready for the visitors? Shall I brush your whiskers?'

'Prrr-rr . . . Prrr-rr . . . Prrr-rr . . .' sang Alfie as he weaved in and out of Fred's legs.

Brown, the Booking Clerk, came on duty. He eyed the grey and white striped cat admiringly. 'My word, Alfie,' he said. 'You're a credit to the station.'

'Miaow!' said Alfie, thinking how jolly everyone was this morning. Long might it last!

Alfie was kept busy for the next two hours, seeing passengers in and out of trains. He always remembered to stand well back from the platform edge when express trains approached. Now and then he ran to the front of the station to see if there was any sign of the children.

'Impatient!' laughed Fred. 'It's not nearly time yet.'

But soon it *was* time and Alfie took up his position to greet the children. His head jerked from side to side and his ears twitched.

Then he heard a murmur of voices and round a corner came a crocodile of children and two teachers. Some of the children were carrying pencils and notebooks, some

pencils and drawing pads. They pointed and shouted when they saw Alfie.

'Alfie's there!'

'He's waiting for *us*.'

'He'll show us round the station.'

'I'm sure he's capable of doing that,' laughed one of the teachers.

Hack passed on his way home. 'Have a good time,' he called.

Alfie ran back into the station and miaowed loudly outside the booking office. Brown opened the door. Alfie entered and leapt up on to a wide counter in front of the glass partition. He sat down beside the ticket machine. As the children filed into the hall, they saw Alfie peering at them through the glass circle which had SPEAK HERE underneath. The children surged forward.

'Ticket to Edinburgh, please,' cried one boy.

'Ticket to Newcastle . . .'

'Ticket to Penzance . . .'

'Ticket to Llanfairpwllgwyngyllgogerychwyrndrobwllllantysiliogogogoch!' shouted a Welsh boy.

'Now then, that's enough,' said a teacher, with a smile. 'We're here to learn how the station is run, not to play games.'

'Alfie evidently thinks you should be shown round the booking office first, so follow me,' said Fred.

Inside Brown said to a boy, 'Order a ticket to anywhere – single, return, weekend, just choose.'

'First class day return ticket to London, please,' said the boy promptly.

Just at that moment Alfie, still on the counter, stretched out a paw and accidentally touched several keys on the ticket machine. Brown then pressed another key and out of the top of the machine emerged a single ticket – to Glasgow!

Everyone laughed and Fred said, 'Stop interfering, Alfie.'

Brown demonstrated the *correct* way to issue a first class day return to London. The children were interested in everything. They made notes, sketched and asked lots of questions.

Next, Alfie led the way to Fred's office. There the timetables were examined, and the teleprinter revealed that one train was running late and another one had been cancelled. Fred glanced at the wall clock. 'Who would like to make an announcement to the passengers?' he asked.

'You, Jim,' said a teacher nodding at a boy.

Fred showed Jim how to operate the Public Address System. The boy pressed the TALK key and spoke into the microphone,

'THE 10.22 TRAIN TO BRISTOL WILL BE

89

ARRIVING SHORTLY AT PLATFORM NUMBER ONE.'

Then the boy pressed the CANCEL key.

'Very good,' said Fred. 'I'm sure you could be heard all over the station. Now I'll show . . .'

He was interrupted by a cry of, '*I* want a go,' and before anyone realized his intentions, a boy pushed forward, jabbed at the TALK key and yelled.

'FIRE! FI–'

As Fred thrust the boy aside, Alfie spied a mouse lurking behind a book on the desk.

Fred started to speak quickly, but calmly, into the microphone, 'CHARGEMAN SPEAKING. THERE IS NO–'

Alfie sprang on to the desk and knocked the instrument over. Fred grabbed it, 'GET OFF, ALFIE. *GET OFF!*' he yelled. Then, 'SORRY, PASSENGERS. I REPEAT – THERE IS NO FIRE. NO NEED FOR–'

The mouse disappeared. Alfie jumped on to Fred's shoulders and put his front paws on Fred's head, while his eyes searched the room for it.

'ALFIE!' shrieked Fred. 'SORRY, PASSENGERS. THERE IS NO FIRE. NO NEED FOR PANIC. THE 10.22 TRAIN FOR BRISTOL IS APPROACHING.' Fred was quite breathless.

The mouse scurried down a leg of the desk and, with Alfie in pursuit, dashed on to the platform. Fred followed. All was confusion. The mouse evaded Alfie as it weaved its way between the legs of bewildered passengers. People jumped out of the way as Alfie chased the mouse and Fred tried to catch Alfie.

'Come here, Alfie!' he shouted.

But Alfie turned a deaf ear. The train drew in. By this time Alfie had again lost sight of the mouse but, suddenly, he saw it clinging to a man's trousers. Alfie moved quickly. Too late! Man and mouse had boarded the train. Doors were slammed, a signal given and the train left.

Alfie watched it depart. He hoped the passengers would enjoy having a mouse with them! After all, it wasn't the railway cat's fault if a mouse decided to go on a train journey, was it?

Fred was still breathing heavily as he gazed down at Alfie. '*Alfie*,' he got out at last. 'I'm surprised at you.' Then he relaxed and grinned. 'It *is* one of your duties to keep the station mouse-free. But watch your step!'

'Miaow!' said Alfie. He was glad Fred understood, and he would be on his best behaviour – for a time at least!

Fred led the way back into the office. The offending boy had been sent home.

'Disgraceful behaviour!' said an embarrassed teacher.

'Well, no real harm has been done,' said Fred. 'Don't let it spoil the morning for the others.'

The children spent another profitable hour at the station. When it was time for them to leave, they thanked Fred and made a fuss of Alfie.

'Can we come again?' they wanted to know.

'Of course,' said Fred.

'Miaow!' added Alfie.

He sat beside Fred on the forecourt and watched the children depart.

'Well, it's back to work for me,' said Fred as he bent down to stroke Alfie.

There was no sign of Hack. Alfie hoped Punch had arrived home, in time to win the race. It had been an

exciting but exhausting morning for the railway cat. Time for a nap. The staff-room door was open. He went in, curled up in a chair and closed his eyes.

As he dozed off he wondered whether the mouse was enjoying the train journey to Bristol, and if it would be able to find its way back to the station.

## 2

# Punch in the Race

Alfie was in the middle of a beautiful dream about a fish supper, when he was roused by a rustling and fluttering noise on the roof. He opened one eye, twitched an ear and listened. Sleep overcame him – but not for long. The noise began again.

Nuisance, thought Alfie. Must be a bird – a pigeon, perhaps. A *pigeon*! He'd forgotten about Punch and the race. Could it possibly be Punch on the roof? If so, why was the silly bird losing valuable time, when he should be speeding back to Hack's garden loft to be checked in?

Alfie dashed out of the staff room. In one bound he reached the top of the cycle shed and from there had easy access to the flat roof. There he saw a pigeon, dark blue colour above and white underneath, with a rubber ring round one leg. It was undoubtedly Punch.

From his high vantage point, Alfie could see Hack – and Digby – waiting in the garden. Their heads were raised as they gazed hopefully into the sky for a sight of the homing pigeon. They didn't glance in the station direction, or they might have seen Punch strutting about on the staff-room roof. Alfie was amazed that the bird could be so stupid.

Well, here was a wonderful opportunity for Alfie to get into Hack's good books – for a change! He would chase Punch off the roof towards the pigeon loft. How grateful Hack would be when his eyes roved towards the station and saw what Alfie was doing. Fred would be pleased too, when he heard about it.

Alfie crouched low, tensed his muscles – and sprang! Punch flapped his wings in defiance and rose into the air, where he hovered just out of Alfie's reach. With a great effort Alfie leapt higher, but still Punch evaded him. Alfie was baffled. He sat down again. Punch alighted on the far edge of the roof. Warily they gazed at one another.

Fred looked up from the platform. 'Whatever are you doing on the roof, Alfie?' he called. 'Come down at once.'

'Miaow!' said Alfie, without turning his head. Fred must understand that the railway cat was on important business.

On his stomach, Alfie began to sidle up to Punch. Nearer and nearer he got. Suddenly, he jumped and managed to take a couple of gentle swipes at Punch.

95

And to Alfie's relief, the pigeon, making loud cooing noises, flew off – in the right direction.

Punch would win the race. Hack had probably noticed what had happened on the roof and Alfie would get due credit.

But Alfie's joy was short-lived. Punch made a wide circle, and returned to the roof! And each time Alfie chased him off, the bird flew round in circles – and then came back.

Alfie was feeling desperate. Time was passing. At this rate Punch wouldn't have a chance of winning the race. Hack would return to work with a frown on his face. So Alfie pretended to get very angry. He hissed and snarled at Punch, but the pigeon seemed to be *enjoying* himself. He evidently thought it was a very good game.

And at last, it must be admitted, Alfie began to enjoy himself too. He forgot about the race, about Hack and Digby waiting for Punch. He didn't even stop to think how Fred would react. The game fell into a pattern. Chase Punch, nearly catch him – Punch flies away – returns – it went on and on and on. Alfie had rarely had such fun, and exercise was so good for one!

He took no notice of express trains passing through the station, nor of the hustle and bustle when local trains arrived. But at last he lay down tired out and followed Punch's movements with his eyes. The bird flew round and round for a time and then, evidently deciding the game was finished, flew off towards the loft.

Alfie came to with a start as he watched Punch drop on to a small landing board and enter the loft through a trap door – far, far too late to win the race.

Hack still stood by the loft. Perhaps it was just as well that the railway cat couldn't see the expression on the Leading Railman's face! Alfie made his way down to the platform where Fred was dealing with some parcels.

'Well, well, well,' he said. 'Turned up at last, have you? I wonder what mischief you've been up to.'

'Miaow!' said Alfie as he rubbed his nose against Fred's shoe.

'Hm-mmm . . . You look far too innocent to be true,' said Fred.

At that moment Hack came towards them. Alfie decided against running away, but he stayed as close to Fred as possible. Fred took one look at Hack's face and raised his eyebrows. 'Didn't Punch win the race after all?' he asked.

'He did not,' replied Hack grimly. 'And all because of Alfie.'

'Because of *Alfie*? Nonsense!' cried Fred.

'It's true. I caught sight of them – too late – on the

staff-room roof, and it's my guess that cat was preventing Punch from flying home.'

*Preventing* – Alfie could hardly believe his ears. After
all his efforts to chase the stupid bird off the roof! He
turned his head and licked the fur on his back.

'Really, Hack, I don't believe . . .' began Fred. He
looked thoughtful. 'Er – I did notice Alfie on the roof,
but there was no sign of Punch.'

'You wouldn't have been able to see him from the
platform,' retorted Hack. 'I'll prove to you that Punch
was there. Wait!'

He strode off down the platform and returned with a
ladder. He quickly climbed up on to the roof, where he
disappeared from view. Soon his head appeared over
the guttering.

'Watch!' he called out. He held out one hand, opened
it, and down floated a few feathers. 'Punch's feathers!'

'Well, er . . . er – I see what you mean,' said Fred.

Fortunately just then, a train drew up at the
platform.

'Back to business,' called Fred, with relief. 'Come
down, Hack. You're on duty now.'

Alfie made himself especially pleasant to the passengers, doing his best to greet each one individually. In
return he received nods, smiles and an occasional stroke
or pat.

After the train had left, Hack said stubbornly, 'You *must* admit, Fred – Punch lost because of Alfie.'

'But Alfie always plays games chasing your pigeons away,' said Fred.

'Games! Huh!' cried Hack. 'Well, he's just had a very expensive game. And if he doesn't keep well away from my birds in future, I'll . . . I'll . . .'

'Oh, come now, Hack,' said Fred. 'I'm sure Alfie didn't mean any harm, even if it was his fault – which I doubt.'

'Miaow!' said Alfie. Good old Fred!

'I'm sorry Punch didn't win,' Fred went on, 'but, never mind, Hack, perhaps *Digby* will make up for it. I hear you've entered him for the Dog Championship at the County Show.'

Hack nodded. 'I'm sure Digby has a chance of winning the Cup this year,' he said more cheerfully. 'So long as that cat keeps his nose out of my affairs.'

Fred laughed. 'Alfie couldn't possibly do anything to prevent Digby winning,' he said.

'Wouldn't trust him,' muttered Hack, with a sidelong glance at Alfie, who growled just a little in his throat. 'As a matter of fact,' Hack went on, 'I've been thinking . . .'

'Miaow!' interrupted Alfie (rather rudely)!

'. . . it would be much better if we kept a dog, instead of a cat, on the station.'

'A *dog*,' cried Fred, astonished. 'What on earth would we want with a dog when we've got Alfie?'

'Well, for a start, dogs are more intelligent than cats . . .' began Hack.

'Brr-r . . . brr-r . . . brr-r . . .' grumbled Alfie. He didn't like the sound of this.

'. . . take Digby, for example.'

*Digby*, thought Alfie. That floppy-eared creature intelligent? Good for a lark now and then was Digby, and affectionate – but intelligent? Alfie shook his head.

'Digby?' repeated Fred. 'Huh! Give me Alfie any time.' He stroked Alfie from the top of his head down to the end of his tail. 'Make no mistake, Hack, there will be no Digby – or any other dog – on this station. And, what's more, I'd like to see Digby do anything Alfie can't do.'

'Cats!' muttered Hack, with a shrug, as he went off over the bridge.

Fred laughed out loud and Alfie rolled on to his back. He couldn't imagine how Digby would manage to keep rats and mice away from the station. Nor how he would have the patience to see trains in and out and be friendly to the passengers all the time. There was much more to being the railway cat than one would think.

'Do try and behave yourself, Alfie,' said Fred as he went into his office and closed the door. The door reopened and Fred's head appeared. His eyes twinkled. 'But, don't worry,' he said. 'I wouldn't change you for all the Digbys in the world!' Fred's head disappeared and the door closed again.

Alfie walked out of the station with his head and tail held high. Trust Fred to stick up for him. Still, Alfie felt just a little bit guilty. Had he tried hard enough to send Punch home in time to win the race?

He sat down outside the station. While he kept his eyes and ears open for anything interesting, he wondered how he could please Hack by helping Digby to win the Cup.

He *must* think of a way.

He strolled down the road and stopped outside Hack's garden gate. Digby soon scented Alfie and dashed round from the back of the house. The dog yelped and barked loudly as he jumped up and down against the gate in his efforts to get at Alfie.

Alfie felt very superior as he sat and stared at Digby through the bars. He, Alfie, might be only a cat (according to Hack!) but he was never fenced in like Digby. Fancy being unable to take a walk whenever one felt like it, even at midnight – or retire into a corner of the station when one wanted to be quiet.

Alfie wouldn't choose a cooped-up dog's life for anything. But, back to the question in mind. How was he going to help Digby to win the Cup?

Leaving the dog to his now frenzied barking, Alfie, deep in thought, returned to his station duties. He'd start watching right away for an opportunity to help Digby.

He hadn't long to wait.

# 3

# The Obedience Class

The very next Saturday morning when Alfie was sunning himself outside the station, Hack, who was off duty, came down the road with Digby on a lead.

Odd, thought Alfie. Hack and Digby usually went the other way up to the five-acre field for a walk and a romp – not often enough though, thought Alfie.

Fred appeared. ''Morning, Hack,' he called. 'Taking Digby shopping?'

'Er, yes – well, no,' said Hack. 'As a matter of fact we're going to the obedience class in the village hall.'

'*Obedience* class!' exclaimed Fred. 'For you or for Digby?'

'*Dog* obedience class,' said Hack, glaring at Fred. 'Not that Digby needs instruction,' he added hastily. 'He's just going along for a refresher course – to keep him in trim for the Show.'

Fred raised his eyebrows. Hack jerked the lead as Digby edged towards Alfie. 'Come on, Digby,' he said. Off they went with Digby straining at the lead.

'I'd like to be in the hall this morning,' said Fred with a grin.

'Miaow!' agreed Alfie. He'd already decided to go along to the hall – might learn something useful. Alfie always preferred to please himself what he did, but he wasn't going to miss an opportunity of watching Digby in training and, if possible, finding a way of helping him.

Alfie made his way through back gardens and over fences to the hall, where he jumped up on to a sill and gazed through a window. The dog trainer was arranging chairs in a wide circle. The man left the hall and, quick as a flash, Alfie was through the partly-open window. Then, with a couple of leaps and a scramble, he reached a high shelf. He lay down behind two piles of books, from where he had a very good view of the hall through a gap between the books.

The trainer returned and gradually the hall began to fill with owners and dogs.

'Take a seat everyone,' called the trainer.

Alfie kept a sharp look-out for Digby. Ah, yes, there he was, pulling so hard on the lead that Hack fairly shot through the doorway into the hall.

Soon every seat was occupied by a dog owner. Alfie counted at least seven different breeds of dogs. He recognized the butcher's long-haired hound and old

Mrs Taylor's dumpy Pekinese and a few others – and, of course, Digby.

There was a great deal of yapping and barking, even whining (to Alfie's disgust) from some of the dogs until the trainer put up a hand.

'Quiet, please – quiet,' he cried. Gradually there was a hush as owners managed to control their pets.

'Now we'll begin . . .' said the man.

But just then Digby looked up at the shelf and started howling. He jumped about and pulled a red-faced Hack right off his chair.

Digby *knows* I'm here – now that shows intelligence, thought Alfie.

'Please restrain your dog, Mr Hack,' said the trainer.

Hack did his best and the instruction began. A small dog and its owner went into the middle of the ring. The trainer held the lead. 'Walk!' he ordered. The dog looked up at him, got the message, walked alongside the man, and after that obeyed nearly every command.

Very good, thought Alfie. He hoped Digby would do as well. Each dog had a turn. Some were quick to learn, others had to be coaxed and told what to do over and over again.

Really, thought Alfie! Fred had only to tell him anything *once* and he understood what was required. How much more intelligent cats were than dogs.

Digby was very uneasy as he awaited his turn. He constantly glanced up at the shelf and occasionally gave a short, sharp bark. Once he sprang up and pulled on the lead.

'Down, Digby – *down*!' hissed Hack as he pushed the dog flat on the floor.

Poor Digby, how undignified, thought Alfie.

And then it was Digby's turn. Hack led him into the ring. Alfie felt very excited. He must watch carefully. He leaned forward and – to his horror! – a pile of books slid off the shelf and fell to the floor with a crash. Alfie found himself in full view of everyone. In a panic, he took a flying leap off the shelf and fled into a corner.

'It's Alfie!' yelled Hack, exasperated, whereupon Digby pulled him right off his feet and dragged him along the floor.

'Oh! Ow! Ouch!' shouted Hack as his elbow hit the floor. Pandemonium broke out as all the dogs started barking. Digby managed to reach Alfie, who boxed him across the nose. The dog drew back, but unexpectedly launched another attack. Taken by surprise, Alfie scratched Digby's nose.

Oh – I didn't *mean* to do that, he thought guiltily.

The trainer grabbed Alfie and held him in his arms. He waited while Digby had a plaster put on his nose then, still holding Alfie, he addressed the class.

'Dogs must be trained to get used to cats, to treat them with respect,' he said, with a long stare at the unfortunate Hack.

'Miaow!' said Alfie, very pleased with this statement.

The man looked down at him. 'And there's no need for you to be afraid of dogs, Alfie,' he said.

'Miaow?' said Alfie again. Afraid of dogs? Me? Not likely. He rubbed his head under the man's chin.

'You'd better sit down quietly somewhere until we've finished,' said the man.

Alfie jumped down and sat upright by the trainer, with his front paws side by side. He looked up at the man as if to ask, What about *my* training?

The trainer looked surprised. 'I'll guarantee this cat could show your dogs a thing or two,' he said to the class. 'Come on, Alfie – walk!'

Always willing to oblige, thought Alfie, as he trotted beside the man all the way down the long hall and back again.

'Stay!' was the next order, as the trainer put out a hand and went off down the hall on his own.

That's easy, thought Alfie. He stayed.

'Come!' was the next command and, waving the tip of his tail, Alfie galloped towards him. This *was* a good game, almost as enjoyable as the one he'd had with Punch. He must encourage Fred to join in.

'Good cat. *Good* cat!' said the trainer. 'He's an example to all. Now we'll have the next dog, please.'

Alfie sat down in the corner again and watched Digby put through his paces. Digby didn't show to advantage. He went plod-plod-plod down the hall instead of walking briskly, and he refused to come when called.

Suddenly Alfie had an inspiration. He *knew* now what was wrong with Digby. The dog was out of condition. He needed far more exercise than Hack gave him. Now Alfie realized how he could help Digby to win the Cup – get him to take more exercise. Alfie was determined that somehow – he didn't yet know *how* – he would see that Digby was encouraged to run and run – and run!

Soon the class was dismissed and dogs and owners left the hall. Alfie followed at a safe distance behind Hack and Digby. Fred was outside the station. Alfie rushed up and weaved in and out of Fred's legs. 'Prrr-rr . . . Prrr-rr . . . Prrr-rr . . .' he sang.

As Hack and Digby came up Fred called out, 'Had a good morning, Hack – Digby do well?'

Hack didn't answer and then Fred noticed the plaster on Digby's nose. 'Oh, dear,' he said. 'Whatever . . . ?'

'That cat can't keep his claws to himself,' burst out Hack.

'That's not true,' said Fred firmly. 'Alfie *never* uses his claws unless he's provoked.'

'Miaow!' said Alfie. In any case, it was only a surface scratch – hardly drew blood. It would heal long before the Show.

Digby broke loose and, with his mouth wide open, rushed up to Alfie. He stopped short within an inch or two of Alfie's nose. What good sharp teeth he's got, thought Alfie admiringly. They'll help to win him marks at the Show. He sat and stared at Digby without blinking once.

Fred came to the rescue. 'Now then, you two,' he said. 'You'll have to learn to live peaceably as neighbours.'

'Miaow!' But we *do* – why can't they understand?

'Woof! Woof! Woof!' agreed Digby.

'Alfie couldn't live peaceably with anyone,' cried Hack.

'Nonsense! I agree Alfie can be, well, er . . . mischievous at times,' said Fred. 'But he's still the most friendly and intelligent cat on the whole railway system.'

'You don't know what you're talking about,' said Hack. 'Come on, Digby.' Off they went home.

When they were out of sight Fred wagged a finger at Alfie. 'Really, Alfie!' he said. 'Digby can be an excellent dog, you know. He could be very intelligent if he tried a bit harder – and if Hack didn't give in to him so much *and* – most important – if he had more exercise.'

'Miaow!' said Alfie. Digby *was* going to have much more exercise, come what may.

'Keep out of Digby's way until after the Show,' ordered Fred.

Keep out of Digby's way? That was the very last thing Alfie intended. He'd got to work hard on Digby to get some of the fat off him.

'Saucer of milk, Alfie?' said Fred.

'Miaow!' Please!

They went into the staff room together. Fred stayed and had a cup of tea while Alfie drank the milk. Life could be very pleasant when one had an understanding friend like Fred around, thought the railway cat.

# 4

# The Chase

It was only two weeks to the County Show. I *must* get busy with Digby right away, thought Alfie. Next day, when Hack was on duty, he noticed Mrs Hack, with a basket over one arm, going past the station on her way to the village. It had been raining but the sky had cleared and the sun was peeping through the clouds. There was a good chance that Digby would have been given the run of the garden.

Off ran the railway cat up the road. He jumped up on to the high wall enclosing Hack's garden, where he stopped short in surprise. Hack had lined the top of the wall with barbed-wire entanglements – to keep out cats, including Alfie!

What a lark, he thought, as he carefully stepped over the wire from one end of the wall to the other, without as much as scratching a toe-nail. He'd show Hack what cats were made of!

He could see Digby stretched out by the kitchen door, watching him. Punch and the other pigeons were asleep in their loft against the far wall. Alfie leapt on to a convenient tree branch overhanging the garden and sat down. Digby got up and rushed across the lawn. He stood on his hind legs scratching at the tree trunk with blunt claws, while Alfie sat calmly on the branch above his head. What a good thing dogs were unable to climb trees, thought Alfie.

He got up, yawned and stretched himself. Just then another cat appeared on the wall. Digby turned his head and, quick as lightning, Alfie slid down the trunk and landed in the garden – in Digby's own territory. He ran. After him came Digby. Round and round they sped, through the flower beds and the vegetable patch, across the lawn, round to the front of the house and back again, churning up mud as they went.

They had a strenuous time, stopping only now and then for a brief rest. What excellent exercise Digby was having, thought Alfie. If they could only do this every day until the Show, the dog would be as fit as a fiddle.

Alfie pricked up his ears as the garden gate clicked. Mrs Hack had returned. Time to go. Back at the station he slipped into the staff room and curled up in a chair. It was hard work getting Digby into condition, he thought, as he closed his eyes.

Hack came in. 'Huh! Tired out so early in the day?' he remarked. 'Up to no good, I suppose – as usual.'

'Miaow!' said Alfie indignantly, without opening his

eyes. *You'll* never guess what I've been doing for Digby.

But Hack guessed as soon as he saw the condition of his garden. Flowers and vegetables uprooted, grass flattened and mud everywhere. He dashed back to the station and ran into the staff room to see Fred. Alfie slept on.

'That cat's been in my garden tantalizing Digby,' he stormed. 'I'll keep him out. You'll see. I'll teach him a lesson . . . I'll . . .'

There's no peace, sighed Alfie, as he opened one eye to look at Hack. Really, the man was beside himself. What a fuss about damage to a garden when there were far more important matters to be considered – Show Day, for instance.

When Hack, muttering to himself, had left, Fred picked Alfie up and put him on a table. 'No use struggling,' he said firmly. All Alfie wanted just then was sleep, and more sleep.

'Um . . . just look at the state of your fur. *Alfie*, you disobedient cat – you *have* been in Hack's garden!'

'Miaow!' agreed Alfie. And you'd thank me if you knew why I've been there.

'Well, I'm going to give you a thorough clean-up,' said Fred. 'And make sure you stay clean. You've got to be in good trim for . . . never mind what.'

'Miaow?' said Alfie, puzzled. Never mind *what*?

Fred opened a cupboard, took out a brush and comb and began to groom Alfie. He brushed and combed until the railway cat felt that every hair on his body and every whisker on his face had been dealt with. My word, Fred had really got a bee in his bonnet about cleanliness. This must be what was meant by spring cleaning! Or perhaps the Area Manager was due to inspect the station?

Fred finished at last. He pulled Alfie's ears gently. 'See you stay away from Hack's garden – or I'll lock you in the staff room,' he threatened.

But nothing was going to stop Alfie from visiting Digby. He never missed a single opportunity of dropping into the garden and allowing Digby to chase him. Once or twice Hack caught them at it. Each time he shouted and shook his fist as Alfie made a hasty retreat. But Alfie returned time after time. Fred tried locking him up, but he always managed to escape.

But the railway cat was worried. Digby was certainly thinner – well he might be! – but in Alfie's opinion the dog still panted too much. His lungs had not yet had enough exercise. It was now Thursday, only two more days to the Show.

Alfie thought about the matter all day. During that night when he was patrolling the station, he heard a

loud clanging noise outside. The station dustbin lid! He
stood still, with ears raised and one paw held high.
There wasn't any wind so who, or what, had knocked
off the lid? Then there was a scuffling sound.

Cats, guessed Alfie. Greedy, overfed domestic cats
with nothing better to do than raid dustbins for odd
scraps of food they didn't need. He'd see them off!

He made his way out of the station. To his surprise
there wasn't a cat in sight but, clearly visible in the
moonlight, was Digby fighting a large rat for possession
of the dustbin. (However had Digby managed to get out
of the house, wondered Alfie?)

Alfie settled down in a corner and watched. Should he
join in the fray? Then a better idea struck him. Here was
a golden opportunity, perhaps the last, to get Digby on
the run. He crept up stealthily behind Digby and let out
an ear-splitting, 'MIAOW-MIAOW-MIAOW . . .
AOW . . . AOW . . .'

Digby jumped and turned round. Alfie spat at him,
then dashed off down the village street. Digby aban-
doned the dustbin to the rat and raced after him. Down
the street they ran, turned left and followed a bridle
path as far as the gravel pit. Round and round – and
round! – the pit they sped, then back to the road and
right through some roadworks and sticky tar into the
main street again.

Alfie was beginning to feel exhausted. Now *he* was panting! He glanced back to see Digby, looking quite fierce, still pounding after him. Oh, dear! Alfie hoped his friend realized this was for his own good – and supposed to be fun as well.

But Digby was gaining ground – he was far too close for comfort. As they went past the church Alfie remembered having noticed the steeplejack at work high up on the church spire during the day. He swerved and, managing to evade Digby, jumped the gate leading into the churchyard. To his relief he saw the steeplejack's ladders still in position. He took a flying leap on to the bottom rung of a ladder and quickly made his way upwards until he reached a second ladder, which led him right to the top of the spire.

Behind him Digby scrambled on to the first ladder, but his weight pulled it from its moorings and it crashed to the ground. From his high perch Alfie watched as Digby, tail between his legs, ran off homewards.

To Alfie the ground seemed a low way off. However was he going to get down? Carefully he stretched out on the ledge below the weathercock. He was thankful it was a calm, clear night. A wind at this moment would be his worst enemy.

If he hadn't felt so insecure he would have admired the view all round. Hearing a familiar sound he raised his head, and soon a train – the late-night express from Bristol – rushed under the road bridge and through the station on its way to London. How Alfie wished he was on the train instead of being stranded on top of the church spire.

He started when he heard a faint noise far below. He looked down. To his amazement he saw two white-clad figures emerge from the church. Alfie's fur stood on end and he trembled with fright. Ghosts! No doubt about that. What other white figures would be coming out of a church at nearly midnight?

Alfie feared the ghosts would catch sight of him, float to the top of the spire and . . . and . . . and . . . he couldn't bear to imagine what might happen to him. He moved nervously and nearly fell off the ledge.

'*Miaow!*' he moaned.

The two figures looked up.

'It's a cat!' exclaimed one ghost.

'It's no ordinary cat – it's our Alfie,' shouted the other ghost.

*Not* the other ghost, for Alfie had immediately recognized *Hack's* voice. He sighed with relief – but whatever was the stupid man doing at midnight looking like a ghost? Anyhow, it explained why Digby was out at night on his own. The dog must have escaped from the house to follow his master.

Hack went on shouting, 'I give up my sleep to do a voluntary rushed job to decorate the church in time for the festival and what do I find? Alfie up to mischief again!'

'Well, it's no use grumbling. We'll have to get him down somehow,' said the other man. 'What about sending for the steeplejack?'

'That would take far too long – he lives about ten miles away. Much better to send for the fire brigade. I'll go and rouse the vicar and use his phone. You open the gate for the brigade.'

Off went a much displeased Hack. He returned with the vicar and very soon a siren was heard in the distance and the fire engine arrived. It turned into the church-yard and drew up at the church door. By this time several villagers, disturbed by the commotion, had arrived on the scene.

The firemen jumped down and immediately began to uncoil the hoses. 'Where's the fire?' one shouted.

'There's no fire,' cried Hack. 'It's Alfie, up there.' He pointed.

'Alfie? Alfie who? Oh, you mean *Alfie*, the railway cat. That won't do. Trains wouldn't run without him on duty. We'll soon have him down.'

He looked up at the spire. 'We'll use the aerial ladder,' he decided.

Alfie watched as the ladder emerged from a chassis on the engine and started to rise, up and up and up until it stopped right in front of him. Swiftly the fireman climbed up to the top of the ladder and grabbed Alfie.

'Miaow . . . aow . . . aow . . . !' cried Alfie as he snuggled up against the man's jacket for the downward trip.

Everyone, except Hack, clustered round to make sure the railway cat was uninjured, but Hack called out, 'Get back to the station, Alfie, and look for mice – that's your job, not climbing church steeples.'

'Brrr . . . rrr . . . rrr . . .' growled Alfie. Silly man. He thinks I climbed up there on purpose, does he? Nevertheless, to avoid further trouble, Alfie strolled back to the station.

Next morning Fred came along to the staff room. I've heard all about your little escapade, Alfie,' he cried. 'Let me have a look at you.'

Oh, no, not *another* grooming, groaned Alfie to himself. Whatever was the matter with Fred – his best friend – always wanting to clean him up, day after day after day. Surely spring cleaning didn't go on for ever?

But Fred was determined. He brushed and combed Alfie and, noticing one or two specks of tar on his fur, produced some cleaning fluid and rubbed and rubbed until there wasn't a trace of the sticky stuff left.

126

As soon as Fred had finished with him Alfie, in high spirits, ran out and rolled over and over in the loose soil on one of the rose beds. Fred came out and shook his fist at him – which surprised Alfie very much. Fred had never done that before.

However, Alfie felt happy. Digby had had lots of exercise last night. There could be no doubt now about him bringing home the Cup on Saturday.

# 5

# Show Day

On Friday night Alfie went to bed far too excited to sleep for thinking about Digby. Next morning he was up long before the London overnight express had passed through the station. For something to do he sat down on the platform and licked himself all over – not that it was necessary after all Fred's efforts to keep him clean!

The express went through the station with a whoosh! and a roar! Alfie made his way to the gate. He knew that Hack had taken a day's leave to go with Digby to the Show. Fred would see to breakfast, thought Alfie, but to his surprise a reliefman was the first to report for duty.

'Miaow?' Alfie said. Where's Fred?

'Ready for breakfast, old chap?' asked the man. 'Well, Fred won't be coming on duty until the evening shift, but don't worry, Brown will soon be here.'

Brown arrived and Alfie hadn't long to wait for his meal. Afterwards he hurried back over the bridge to the Down platform, from where he had no intention of moving until he had watched Digby's departure by the 9.30 local train – a fitter, leaner Digby thanks to his friend, the railway cat! And Alfie also intended being on the Up platform to greet Digby on his return with the silver Cup. It promised to be an exciting day.

Five minutes or so before the train was due Fred, dressed for an outing and carrying a large covered basket, came on to the platform.

He's going fishing, guessed Alfie. Do him good. In Alfie's opinion Fred had been working too hard lately. He rolled over and over at Fred's feet.

'Hey there – stop that, Alfie, you'll get dusty!' cried Fred as he went down and flapped a large handkerchief over Alfie's back, sides and stomach. Alfie enjoyed this but, really, Fred *was* overdoing things.

Digby burst on to the platform pulling Hack after him. Alfie purred with pleasure at the sight of this alert, bright-eyed, slim dog with the glossy coat. Fred bent down to stroke Digby.

'Best of luck, Digby,' he said.

'Woof! Woof! Woof!' barked Digby. He pulled Hack further down the platform – to keep away from Alfie and further trouble? Fred stayed with Alfie and chatted to one or two waiting passengers.

The train was announced and soon drew up at the platform. Doors opened, passengers alighted and Fred stood back to allow others to join the train. Alfie looked up at him. 'Miaow?' he said. Thought you were going fishing?

Just before the train was ready to move off, Fred bent down, lifted Alfie, put him in the basket and closed the lid. Then, holding the basket in front of him, he got into the train.

Alfie was furious. He'd been catnapped once and Fred knew how he hated being shut up anywhere. The railway cat's wailing became louder and louder.

'Shush! Shush!' said Fred as he opened the basket lid and stroked Alfie.

'Miao . . . aow . . . aow . . .' grumbled Alfie. But, after protesting for a good ten minutes he decided to make the best of things. After all, Fred had never let him down yet. He closed his eyes.

'That's better, Alfie,' said Fred soothingly.

It was only a short journey to the town. When the train stopped Fred shut the lid, got off the train and started walking. Alfie enjoyed the slight swinging sensation in time to Fred's footsteps. Soon he could tell that Fred was walking on grass, and he could hear people shouting, and music in the background. Through a slit in the side of the basket Alfie caught sight of a large white tent.

Then it dawned on him! They were on the Show

ground! Alfie felt excited. How kind of Fred. He must be taking him, Alfie, the railway cat, to see his friend Digby win the silver Cup. Now he understood everything; why Fred looked so smart; why he had groomed Alfie to make sure the railway cat looked presentable for his outing. Alfie was sure Fred would let him out of the basket and hold him up to watch Digby in the competition.

But Alfie was wrong. They entered a large marquee. Fred put down the basket, opened the lid and popped Alfie into a small cage, with a metal floor and top and sides of wire. He, Alfie, cooped up in a *cage*! Fred must have gone right out of his mind.

But Fred was smiling as he closed the cage door. 'Now Alfie, just settle down. I'll be near at hand when the judging takes place.'

You could have knocked Alfie down with a feather. Judging what? There wasn't a dog to be seen, although Alfie could distinguish sounds of yapping and barking not far distant. But numbered cages, each with a cat inside, formed a ring round the tent.

Alfie glanced round. All sorts of cats! In one section long-haired cats, in another short-haired cats, in yet another he recognized blue-eyed, sleek-coated Siamese cats – in fact, all breeds of cats, including a group of ordinary-looking cats like Alfie himself.

How could Fred be so foolish as to think of entering Alfie in such a contest? Why, he wouldn't stand a chance against some of these beauties. He, Alfie, was a *railway* cat, not a show cat! He began to worry about Fred.

But Fred said, 'You're Number 14 in the Working Cats section, Alfie, so do your best for the railway.'

Working cats! Well, that was quite a different kettle of fish, thought Alfie. The show manager's voice came over the loud speakers,

'Will all exhibitors leave the tent, please. Judging will now commence.'

'Good luck, Alfie,' said Fred. He waved as he followed other owners out of the tent.

The Siamese cats were first to be judged. Each cat in turn was taken out of its cage and put on the judge's table for examination. It was some time before it was Alfie's turn. He sat very still and quiet during the inspection of teeth, ears, face, paws, nails, whiskers – would the man never finish?

'Miaow!' he said once. I might not be a *pretty* cat, but I know I could win a prize as best mouser or best ratter!

When the judge had finished he whispered into Alfie's left ear, 'Very good, Alfie – extremely well-behaved.'

'Miaow!' said Alfie again. I'm always well-behaved – or nearly always.

Alfie was returned to the cage. By now he was enjoying himself. It was fun being with the other cats with Fred not far away. Several times he wondered how Digby was getting on and whether he, Alfie, would be given a fish supper to celebrate Digby's winning the Cup?

When the last cat had been dealt with, the owners were allowed to return to the tent. Soon the manager's voice was heard again. Starting with the Siamese, he called out the winners in each section. When he came to Working Cats, Fred stood very still, hands in pockets, while Alfie pricked up his ears.

'Winner of the Working Cats section – Number 14. Alfie, the railway cat,' came the announcement.

People clapped and cheered. Fred threw up his arms and waved them about excitedly. 'What do you think of that, Alfie?' he cried. 'You've won a certificate.'

A certificate, thought Alfie. What do I want with that? A whole salmon – or half a salmon – would be more appropriate.

'Now we come to the best *overall* winner – Best Cat in the Show,' the voice continued. There was a pause and Fred shuffled his feet. 'Best Cat in the Show – Number 14 Alfie, the railway cat.'

134

This time Fred was speechless for at least half a minute. Then he burst out, 'You've won a prize, Alfie – a real silver Cup!'

'Miaow!' said Alfie. What did he want with a *Cup*? He wouldn't be able to get his head inside such an object.

He sat on the judge's table again while Fred received the award. Amid laughter, Fred produced a small bottle of milk and filled the Cup. He placed it in front of Alfie, who put his nose in, stuck out his tongue and lapped loudly. Cream! But, to his disgust, as he had thought, he could only reach the top of the cream.

'Never mind, Alfie,' said Fred. 'You can finish it off back at the station.'

That suited Alfie – but fancy winning a useless thing like a silver Cup! He hoped Digby's Cup would be much, much larger! As Fred had to be back on duty by evening, he and Alfie left the Show before they had time to find out how Digby was getting on.

At the station everyone congratulated the railway cat on winning the Cup, which was placed in a locked glass-fronted case on a shelf in the booking office, for all to admire.

While Fred went about his duties, Alfie lay curled up on a station bench to await the arrival of Digby with his trophy. Nothing disturbed the railway cat for the next hour – not the coming and going of passengers, nor the

arrival and departure of trains, but he opened his eyes when Digby's train was due.

Alfie jumped down as Fred came along to meet the in-coming train – with Digby and the Cup aboard! As the passengers left the train, Alfie's head jerked from left to right and from right to left, but there was no sign of the dog. Last but one to alight was Hack, then came Digby.

Digby looked happy enough and when he saw Alfie he lunged forward and jerked the lead out of Hack's hand. Alfie retreated behind Fred. 'Woof! Woof! Woof!' barked Digby as he wagged his tail.

Fred called out, 'Where's the Cup, Hack?'

'No Cup,' said Hack, gloomily. 'Lost a few vital marks for spots of tar on his coat. *Tar* – where did he get that from, I wonder?' He gave Alfie a suspicious glance.

Fred also stared at Alfie, as he eased his cap from his forehead, but all he said was, 'Well, that's a pity, but never mind, Hack, there's another Show in two months' time. Digby is in such good condition I'm sure he's worthy of winning any competition.'

Hack sighed and nodded. Off he went with Digby. Alfie felt very upset. *He* hadn't wanted to win a Cup – Fred shouldn't have entered him in the Show. He stared at his friend reproachfully, then jumped on to the bench, lay down and closed his eyes.

'Don't worry, Alfie,' said Fred. 'That's how it is – but *tar*, now I wonder . . . ?'

Alfie opened one eye.

'. . . and don't look at me with that butter-wouldn't-melt-in-your-mouth expression!'

Alfie got up, turned his back on Fred and lay down again. It was very difficult trying to do the right thing all the time, he thought.

He was soon fast asleep.

# 6

# The Bullion Bag

That night Alfie decided he was in need of fresh air and exercise, so he started off along the top of the railway embankment. At a point not far from the station a lane, bordered by a strong wire fence, ran alongside the railway track for a short distance.

Alfie sat down to wait for the east-bound night parcels train to pass. There was a full moon. The driver would probably see him and wave. He turned his head as he heard a faint sound. A van, without lights, was being driven very slowly along the lane. Alfie lay down flat as the vehicle came to a standstill opposite him. He noticed that the van carried no trade name or other identification. He overheard two men talking.

'Just our luck – it must be running late,' said one man.

'Well, we daren't risk standing here,' said the other man. 'Drive back to the hide-out. We'll wait there ten minutes before returning. It should have passed by then.'

The van did a three-point turn and moved off. Now what could be running late but a train – the parcels train perhaps – thought Alfie? But why were these men so interested in a train?

He resumed his waiting position, but soon another car approached. Goodness, why such activity in the middle of the night? It was getting almost like Piccadilly Circus! This time it was a Panda car with sidelights showing. Alfie was always happy to see his friends the police, so he climbed up the wire fence and balanced on top of one of the concrete support posts. He miaowed loudly.

'Why, hello, Alfie,' called the constable cheerfully. 'You on duty, too?'

The sergeant beside him leaned forward. 'Well, let us know if you see or hear anything suspicious,' he called out.

The car moved off slowly.

Hmmm . . . mm . . . I *could* have told them about the unmarked van, thought Alfie. Soon he heard the parcels train in the distance. As it drew level the driver leaned out of the engine cab and waved to Alfie.

As the guard's van passed, something came flying out of the van window. Alfie ducked and fell off the post. A large bag, which had just missed his head, burst open as it hit the ground. Alfie's eyes widened at the sight of hundreds and hundreds – perhaps *thousands* – of coins, glinting in the moonlight, strewn over the grass.

Could they possibly be *gold* coins? If so, what a lot of fish and cream could be bought with all that money. But what did it all mean, thought Alfie? An unmarked van with no lights – a police car obviously on the alert – money thrown out of a train – was there a connection?

Alfie looked up to see the van coming back. His mind worked quickly. These men must be in league with whoever had thrown the bag out of the train and had come to collect the haul.

But it would take them much longer to pick up the money than they had expected. No doubt they had planned to snatch the bag and be off at full speed. They were going to have a shock.

Alfie decided this was no place for him at the moment. The men might be armed. How could he raise the alarm? Hastily he jumped the fence and streaked off down the lane in the direction of the station. As he passed Hack's house, Digby started to bark.

Alfie stopped short, turned and squeezed under the gate. He sprang on to the kitchen window sill and clawed at the glass with his front paws. Inside, Digby howled and yelped as he jumped on to the sink and tried to get at Alfie through the glass.

Digby made such a commotion that Hack came

stumbling down the stairs and probably thinking there must be an intruder outside, opened the kitchen door. Out shot Digby.

And off the sill leapt Alfie, under the gate and back up the lane. He glanced back to see Digby jump right over the gate. My word, I've never seen him do that before, thought Alfie. What a fit dog he is now!

Alfie reached the van, with Digby not far behind. The two men were on the embankment frantically stuffing handfuls of gold coins into the torn bullion bag and into their pockets. Alfie skidded to a halt but Digby tore past him and, with a howl, fell on one of the men. The other man looked up horrified, ran off, got into the van and with a grinding of gears, drove off. The robber left on the embankment struggled as a snarling Digby, with teeth bared and ears flattened, pressed him to the ground.

Digby is *magnificent* in a crisis, thought Alfie. Suddenly the man exerted all his strength to push Digby away. Alfie wasn't having that. He scrambled down the slope and with claws unsheathed, crashed on top of the man while Digby managed to regain his hold by sinking his teeth into the man's sweater.

'Two of them! Help! Help!' screamed the man, as he fought to get free.

Alfie was beginning to think they wouldn't be able to

restrain the man much longer when he looked up to see his two policemen friends dashing to the rescue. He jumped off the robber and ran behind a tree. Digby couldn't be persuaded to let go of his victim. But soon a breathless Hack arrived and pulled his dog away.

As handcuffs were clapped on to the criminal's wrists, the sergeant said, 'At least we've caught one of the gang, thanks to your SOS, Mr Hack.'

'And thanks also to Digby,' put in the constable. 'You'd both better come along to the police station with us.'

'Here come the reinforcements,' cried the sergeant as another police car drove up.

Alfie watched as Hack and Digby joined the two policemen and the criminal in the first car. It drove off down the lane, leaving the others to guard the bullion.

Alfie went back to the station. As it was such a fine night he settled down on a bench and was soon fast asleep.

He was still there when Fred woke him next morning.

'Come on, lazy bones, breakfast's ready,' cried Fred as he gave the railway cat a playful push.

'Miaow!' said Alfie, as he stretched himself and yawned. Lazy, indeed! *You* don't know what I was up to last night. In the staff room, Alfie listened to Fred and Hack talking about the night's events.

'The criminals hid in the guard's van before the train started, overpowered the guard, tied him up and then threw out the bullion at the appointed place. They escaped from the train when it slowed down at a signal.'

'Well, I hear they've all been rounded up,' said Fred, 'and Digby must be given credit for making the first capture.'

Hack nodded. Then he glanced at Alfie. 'Alfie was there as well. I caught sight of him behind a tree,' he said.

'Not surprised to hear that Alfie had a paw in it,' said Fred, laughing. 'But it was definitely Digby's night, and I reckon he deserves at least a silver Cup, don't you, Alfie?'

'Miaow!' said Alfie. Certainly he does.

Life at the station went on normally for a time. Then one day there was great activity – much cleaning and polishing, weeding of flower beds and washing of platforms and windows. *More* spring cleaning, wondered Alfie – or a station inspection?

That evening Fred brushed and combed Alfie vigorously, a sure sign that something out of the ordinary could be expected. Next morning Alfie was up bright and early.

145

'Area Manager's arriving on the 10.30, Alfie,' Fred called out as he busied himself about the station. At 10.15 Hack went home and returned with Digby. Mrs Hack came along as well, so Alfie knew this was going to be no ordinary inspection. And there were cameramen and reporters on the station.

At 10.15 everyone lined up on the platform as the train came in. Out stepped the Area Manager. Alfie had hoped the VIP had arrived to present a silver Cup to Digby. But the man was carrying only a flat briefcase – and surely a *Cup* wouldn't fit into that? Alfie was *very* disappointed.

And after all Digby didn't receive a Cup. The Manager shook hands with everybody, patted Digby and stroked Alfie. Then he took a small box out of the briefcase, opened the box and held up something round, bright and shining.

'I have great pleasure,' he said, 'in presenting this pure gold medal to Digby, for Animal Bravery in tackling and holding a dangerous criminal.'

The man bent down and fastened the medal on to Digby's collar. Cameras clicked. Digby wagged his tail and barked. Everyone clapped and Alfie miaowed.

After the brief ceremony was over and the Manager had departed, people gathered round to congratulate

Digby and to examine the medal, while Mr and Mrs Hack stood by proudly.

Fred turned to Alfie. 'Everything's turned out well, eh, Alfie?' he said. 'Punch lost the race, but Digby's got a gold medal, so Hack is satisfied.' His eyes twinkled. 'A gold medal is more valuable than a silver Cup isn't it, Alfie?'

'Miaow!' Yes, Alfie supposed it was, but *he* wasn't interested in a Cup or a medal. Next year at the County Show – or the year after, or the year after that – he might try to win a silver *Saucer*. That would be valuable. After all a good-sized saucer could hold a lot of milk – or cream!

Alfie decided to get into training right away. He was never one to let the grass grow under his paws.

# The Railway Cat's
# Secret

# Contents

# 1

# Station Cleaning

Alfie, the railway cat, was disgusted – station cleaning time *again*? And what a cleaning! The staff seemed to have gone berserk. They bustled about as though there wasn't a minute to lose.

Between trains they swept, scrubbed, polished all the furniture and fittings and weeded the flower beds. Passengers alighting from trains were hurried out of the station, while others joining trains were ushered on board without ceremony. All very undignified, thought Alfie, puzzled.

Even Alfie's special friend, Chargeman Fred, had no time for the railway cat. 'Not now, Alfie,' he said firmly, but kindly, as Alfie, miaowing loudly, weaved in and out of the man's legs.

And, 'Clear off, Alfie!' yelled Leading Railman Hack as he tripped and caught his ankle a sharp blow with a broom. (Not my fault this time, thought Alfie!)

But, 'Ouch! Ow . . . don't want to see any more of *you* today,' screamed Hack.

'Brr . . . brr . . . brr . . .' growled Alfie. He never expected any sympathy from Hack.

Brown, the Booking Clerk, popped his head round the office door. 'Phew – such a commotion!' he cried. 'What's it all in aid of?'

'Wish I knew,' said Hack.

'Miaow!' said Alfie. So do I.

Alfie sat down and watched Fred as he darted about the station, giving orders, changing his mind and then charging off somewhere else. It was so unlike his friend to go about tight-lipped, with a frown on his forehead and an air of secrecy about him.

Something clicked in Alfie's mind. Secrecy? That was it. Fred must have a *secret* which he wasn't allowed to tell anyone about – not even the railway cat! Poor Fred. No wonder he looked worried.

Fred came towards him. 'Ah, there you are, Alfie,' he cried (apparently forgetting he had just been ignoring the railway cat). 'I think I'll start on you next.'

Start on me, thought Alfie? That meant only one thing – a good clean. He wasn't going to put up with that if he could help it. He was quite capable of looking after himself, thank you.

So he turned swiftly and, with tail down, set off at a good pace down the platform. Fred followed. 'Come

154

here, Alfie. *Come here*,' he shouted, as he waved his arms.

But leaving the station behind him, Alfie started running along the top of the embankment. He could hear Fred calling, 'Come back, Alfie. Come b . . a . . . c . . . . k . . . .'

Alfie slowed down when Fred was out of earshot, but he went on and on, much further than he had ventured for a long time. Eventually he came to a small wayside station, which had been closed for over a year.

Weeds grew out of cracks on the platform and a rusty gate in a broken-down fence hung askew. Alfie paused to gaze at a small building, once a waiting room and booking office combined. He jumped up on to a sill and looked through a slit in the boarded-up window. Light filtered in from a broken rear window and he could see an old table and a rickety chair.

Wandering round to the back of the station Alfie found what was once a tidy garden, a tangled mass of bushes and weeds. He glanced round in dismay. What a pity. Then he thought – but what a lovely stalking place.

On his stomach he slowly wormed his way through the undergrowth keeping his eyes and ears open all the time. He had gone a short distance when, to his surprise, he emerged into a real garden. A vegetable plot

with neat rows of onions, carrots, cabbages and lettuce, and stakes for peas and beans – quite hidden from view, a secret garden! There was no one in sight.

Who was the gardener? Why was it a *secret* garden? Alfie felt quite excited as he always enjoyed a mystery. He decided to wait and see if anyone turned up. He lay down between two rows of vegetables, but soon became drowsy and fell asleep. After a time he woke up, yawned and stretched himself as he looked round. Still no one about. Very odd.

He left the little station and continued his walk along the embankment. Coming to a tunnel he peered through the opening and saw light streaming in from the other end. When he heard a couple of hoots in the distance he drew back and sat down in the long grass. Soon – with a whoosh! and a roar! – a freight train entered the tunnel, and hooted again as it passed Alfie.

He watched the train until it was out of sight, then he stretched himself lazily and flopped down on his side. He thought about Fred. Was it really necessary for his friend to be so secretive? Why didn't he tell the railway cat about it?

After a time Alfie got to his feet, stretched again and yawned, before deciding he'd better return and see if Fred had calmed down. In any case he was feeling hungry.

So Alfie set off home. As he approached the wayside station he spied a rabbit scampering along the platform. Alfie chased it to the back of the station, and then right through the bushes.

As he emerged into the secret garden Alfie halted to take a quick look round, and lost sight of the rabbit – but no matter, thought Alfie. There was no sign of life in the garden and no sound except for a slight breeze rustling the leaves. It was very eerie, thought Alfie, as he turned and ran all the way back to his own station.

Fred was still busy. So was Hack and everyone else. They ignored Alfie. He tried rubbing a cheek against Fred's leg. Then he stretched up and clawed at his friend's jacket. 'Miaow! Miaow!' he cried. Can't we have a bit of fun?

'*Now* what's the matter, Alfie?' sighed Fred.

'Not getting enough attention, that's what's the matter with him,' put in Hack, scornfully.

'Brr . . . rr . . . rr . . .' howled Alfie.

'Swearing at me again!' cried Hack.

'Don't be ridiculous, Hack!' shouted Fred. 'Feed Alfie and lock him up or we'll never get on.'

Alfie was furious. How could Fred let him down like this? He made a dash down the platform, but Hack lunged forward and grabbed him in a rugby-like tackle.

'Miaow! Miaow! Mi . . ao . . . w . . . .' screeched Alfie as he turned his head and bit Hack's little finger.

'Aargh . . . aargh!' cried Hack as he shook his hand. His grip tightened as Alfie struggled to free himself. Fred came running.

'He bit me!' shouted Hack. 'I'll teach him his manners. I'll train him to . . .'

'Oh, for goodness sake, stop blathering, Hack!' cried Fred. 'Here, give him to me.'

Fred snatched Alfie and carried him into the staff room. He put two bowls on the floor, filled one with raw meat and vegetables and the other with milk. Then he went out, slammed the door behind him, and turned the key in the lock.

And all without a word or a miaow uttered. Alfie couldn't believe it. He was so upset that he ate only half the meat but managed to finish the milk. He spent a very uneasy night and woke long before his usual time. There was a lot more noise than usual when the staff came on duty.

Whatever was going on now? wondered Alfie. No one came to see him, so he howled and howled. When that had no effect he jumped up and rattled the door handle. He did this dozens of times before he heard a key in the lock.

Fred appeared. He shook his head at Alfie. 'Really,

Alfie,' he said. 'Here am I trying to get the station ship-shape for what I hope will be a very happy occasion, while you're making all this fuss and bother.'

'Miaow!' cried Alfie. You're making a lot of fuss and bother yourself.

'If you ask me . . .' began Fred.

'Miaow!' put in Alfie. I didn't.

'. . . I'm fed up with trying to keep a secret,' said Fred, as he banged the table with his fist.

'Miaow!' said Alfie yet again. Surely you could tell me?

'It's like this, Alfie,' Fred went on. 'I've had definite instructions from Headquarters to keep the matter a close secret, as they . . . er . . . er . . . the party concerned, that is, want to spend a nice peaceful time here at the station – incognito, if you get my meaning.'

Alfie didn't understand the last bit, but who was the party concerned? he wondered. Could it be the Lord Mayor? Or the Chancellor of the Exchequer? Or a Pop Group? A Pop Group would be fine. Even Hack would enjoy that.

'Just be seen and not heard today, Alfie,' said Fred. 'To please me.'

Alfie followed him on to the platform, where he stopped short in horror. All was confusion. The *painters* had moved in. Ladders were propped against walls, and doors were being rubbed down before being painted. Alfie shuddered at the thought of paint getting on to his fur and of people ordering him out of the way. There would be no peace.

Fred grew more and more annoyed, as miaowing all the time, Alfie followed him everywhere, up and down platforms, over the bridge and back again and into the office. Whenever Fred stopped Alfie jumped up at him, wanting to play if only for a few minutes.

But Fred refused. 'Alfie, this is just too much,' he raged at last. 'If you can't behave in a sensible manner, I'll have to send you away for a day or two, and you'll miss all the excitement.'

'Miaow!' hissed Alfie. All work and no play was making Fred bad-tempered, but it would take a sledge-hammer to knock sense into his friend's brains just now. Alfie looked behind him at the chaos on the station as, once again, he set off briskly along the top of the embankment – to get away from it all for a time.

He didn't pause at the wayside station. When he came to the tunnel he ran down the embankment and cautiously glanced inside to look again at the circle of light at the far end.

Suddenly, he heard a faint noise inside the tunnel – a bird, perhaps? He listened. All was quiet for a time, then the sound was heard again, very softly, 'Miaow!'

Alfie stiffened in dismay. There must be a *cat* inside the tunnel. How dangerous!

What could he do?

# 2

# The Rescue

Alfie hesitated, then, with a quick glance up and down the lines, he rushed into the tunnel – something he had never done before. It was very gloomy inside, but he could just see stones strewn along the track and he noticed an empty cigarette packet and half a tomato near a shiny rail.

Another faint miaow guided him to a tiny ginger kitten lying in the middle of the fast track. Bending his head Alfie could see that her right foreleg was bent in an unnatural position beneath her body, while her left foreleg was almost touching the rail. The kitten tried to rise but fell back helplessly.

Alfie licked the kitten's shoulder before running back through the tunnel. Instinctively he headed for his own station, but at the little wayside station he stopped, turned, and darted round to the back. He pushed his way through the undergrowth. As he came to the edge of the secret garden he heard someone coughing, 'Hhrraaagh!' He peeped out and saw a man digging.

The man's shirt was torn and his trousers were

hitched up round his knees with string. Must be a tramp, thought Alfie. He miaowed softly. As the tramp turned round Alfie saw that he had a kind, sun-tanned face. However, not observing the railway cat in the bushes, the man shrugged his shoulders and resumed digging.

Alfie crept from under cover. Taking the man by surprise, he wailed loudly, 'M . . I . . . A . . . . O . . . . . W . . . . . . !'

The tramp jumped, dropped his spade and turned round again. 'Why, hello, old chap!' he cried. 'You did give me a fright. Where have you sprung from?' He bent down and stroked Alfie.

Alfie stretched up and pulled hard at the man's trousers with his claws. Then he ran off. After a few yards he stopped and looked round hopefully. 'Miaow!' he cried. Oh, for goodness sake – *come on*!

But the man laughed. 'Sorry,' he said, 'I'm far too busy to play games.'

Alfie rushed back, jumped up nearly pushing the man over before running off again and then stopping. His tail went flick, flick, flick all the time as he waited.

Mystified, the tramp gazed at Alfie. 'Hmmm,' he murmured. 'Wonder what you want? Is something worrying you?'

'Miaow!' cried Alfie. Of course there is!

The man hesitated before deciding to follow Alfie through the bushes and to the tunnel entrance. Alfie set off into the tunnel, but the man shouted, 'Come back. It's not safe in there!'

Alfie returned reluctantly, looked up at the man and said, 'Miaow!' Please understand.

There was silence and then came a faint miaow which echoed eerily in the tunnel. 'My word!' exclaimed the tramp. 'There's a cat in there.' He glanced at his wrist watch. 'Only five or six minutes before the next train is due – just enough time for me to run back for a torch. You wait here.' Alfie watched the man scramble up the embankment and race off towards the secret garden. He returned in a matter of minutes and dashed past Alfie on his way to the kitten.

Alfie waited, his eyes and ears on the alert all the time for the approach of the next train. Would the tramp find the kitten? Would he get her out safely? It seemed a very long time before the man, with the kitten cradled in his arms, stumbled out of the tunnel just as a couple of hoots were heard. He knelt down behind a bush until a train had passed at speed.

'Phew! That was a narrow shave!' he gasped as he got up and wiped his forehead with the back of a hand.

'Miaow!' cried Alfie. Well done!

The kitten miaowed mournfully and closed her eyes.

'Come on,' said the man with a jerk of his head towards the little station. 'Urgent first aid is required.'

He led the way back and entered the waiting room through the rear door. Alfie followed. The man closed the door before gently laying the kitten on her side on the table. Alfie leapt lightly on to the chair to ensure having a good view of the proceedings.

With the utmost care the tramp ran his hands over the kitten's limbs. Once when the kitten jerked in pain he stroked her reassuringly. 'All right. All right,' he said. 'I'll soon put you right.' He turned to Alfie. 'Foreleg fractured in two places,' he said briefly. 'I'll need the first aid box from my secret hiding place in the garden. You stay and keep her company.'

Alfie didn't move an inch until the tramp returned with an armful of articles which he placed on the table. First he filled a saucer with milk from a bottle. 'A drink first!' he cried as he held the saucer in front of the kitten's mouth. Alfie watched eagerly as she feebly put out a pink tongue and managed to lap a little milk.

'She'll be fine soon,' said the man as he opened the small first aid box. Alfie leaned forward, put one paw on the table, and anxiously watched the man's movements.

'Don't worry!' said the man as he gave Alfie a playful push back on to the chair. 'I know what I'm doing – I hold a first aid certificate.'

'Miaow!' said Alfie, relieved to hear that.

'My name's Joe,' the man told Alfie as he started to examine the injured limb. 'I'm down on my luck as I've been out of work for months.' He sighed. 'Trouble is I'm an independent sort of chap – don't want to go on the dole. Rather earn my own living.'

Joe stopped talking as he gave all his attention to the job in hand. Alfie watched intently. Once Joe stretched up and put a hand to his back. 'Ouch!' he cried. 'Wrenched my back pushing too heavy a barrow-load of vegetables. But mustn't grumble. I've been in luck finding this place. I have no right to be here really, so no one – no one, you understand – must find out. It's a secret.'

'Miaow!' said Alfie. You can trust me. Now *I've* got a secret as well as Fred.

Joe went on talking as he dealt with the kitten. 'I'm making just enough money to keep me going, by selling fruit and vegetables in surrounding villages. Haven't got a car but my barrow comes in useful. Wouldn't do to stop a train and ask for a lift, would it?' He laughed.

Alfie rubbed his chin up and down against the table edge to show his appreciation of the joke.

Joe reached for a plaster. 'You know,' he said, 'it's really doing me good to have someone to talk to. It's very lonely here.'

'Miaow!' said Alfie. I'm ready to listen any time.

'Normally I only use this room at night when there's little chance of being found out.' He tapped the table and pointed at the chair. 'An old table, a chair and a camp-bed which I bring in at night make a home for me.'

Joe was silent for a time as he carefully bound up the patient's leg. When he had finished he stood back and gazed at the kitten. 'There now – finished!' he said triumphantly. 'She'll be quite all right in a week or two. Meanwhile I'll have to hide her in the garden during the day, but she can come in here with me at night. But heaven knows what I'm going to give her to eat!' He rubbed the soft fur under the kitten's chin. 'Listen!' cried Joe. 'I can hear her purring.'

'Miaow!' cried Alfie, delighted. So can I.

'Wonder what her name is?' mused Joe. 'I think I'll call her Tansy – a herb I've been planting in the garden this morning. What do you think?'

'Miaow!' agreed Alfie. It suits her.

'Back to gardening,' said Joe. 'There's an extra mouth to feed now, so I'll have to work harder to earn more money.' He picked up Tansy and went outside. Alfie jumped off the chair and followed. 'What about you – have you got some business to attend to?'

'Miaow!' replied Alfie. Yes. Time I went to see how

Fred's getting on without me. The fact that he had a secret made Alfie feel important and on level terms with Fred.

He looked up at Tansy in Joe's arms and then rolled over and over at Joe's feet. The man laughed as Alfie got up and set off at a steady trot towards his own station.

'I'll plant some catmint for you,' Joe called after him.

Alfie glanced back. 'Miaow!' he cried. Good – I'll be back!

# 3

# Hack's Secret

Alfie slowed down before entering the station. He could hear Fred shouting and caught sight of Hack slouching about the platform, while the painters' brushes went swish, swish, swish across the wooden platform seats.

He sat down undecided. Should he turn back? No! The railway cat must be on duty. Warily he walked into the station. 'Miaow!' he greeted waiting passengers. I'm back.

'Hello!' said one man. 'Mind they don't paint you by mistake.'

'Miaow!' said Alfie. That's what I'm afraid of!

Fred bore down on him. 'I've been searching everywhere for you,' he cried reproachfully. 'I'm going to give you a good grooming . . .'

This was too much for Alfie. He started to run.

'Disobedient cat – come back!' yelled Fred, as he stood with arms akimbo and watched the railway cat weave his way between the passengers' legs. Alfie swerved to avoid Hack, but the Leading Railman moved quickly.

'Got you!' he shouted as he swooped and grabbed him by the tail.

'Mia . . ow . . . ow . . . . !' screeched Alfie as he struggled and scratched.

'Oh, no, you don't – not this time – you lazy, good-for-nothing animal,' roared Hack as he shook Alfie. 'Do you know, I actually saw a rat – a *rat*, do you hear? – on Number 1 platform this morning. Where's your sense of responsibility, your loyalty to the railway, your . . . ?'

But Alfie had heard enough. With a mighty struggle he freed himself and jumped down on to the platform with a thud. Where could he take refuge? In this confusion he barged into a ladder and nearly toppled a painter.

'Watch where you're going!' shouted the man, while Hack could be heard calling, 'Catch him – catch him!'

Looking round wildly for an escape route, Alfie saw the booking-office door ajar. He streaked in and crouched underneath Brown's high stool. Brown appeared to be the only calm member of staff. He looked down.

'Hello, Alfie,' he said. 'Trying to avoid the turmoil? Don't blame you. Fred's secret is getting on everybody's nerves.'

'Miaow!' agreed Alfie quietly. *But I've got a secret too.*

Playfully, Brown dangled a piece of string over Alfie's nose. Alfie took a couple of swipes at it and missed.

The door was flung wide open. In came Hack. 'Seen anything of that cat?' he asked. 'Fred wants him.'

'Really?' said Brown innocently. 'Try the car park. Alfie usually patrols there once or twice a day.' Brown glanced through the open door and noticed painters moving ladders.

'Painters finished already?' he asked.

'No, worse luck,' said Hack. 'Fred's ordered them to go down the line to the old wayside station and slap paint on the front of the waiting room – front only he told them. They're to ignore the back.' Hack shook his head. 'Don't know what's come over Fred since he started on this secret lark.'

Alfie flattened his ears in horror. The painters might discover Joe, and Tansy, and the secret garden – and it wouldn't be a secret any longer. He waited impatiently for Hack to go.

But the man lazed against the door. 'You'd think Fred was expecting a visit from royalty the way he's going on,' he said, with a sneer.

'Heavens, no!' laughed Brown. 'We'd have been

advised of such an important event months, even years, ahead.'

'Well, it must be the General Manager, at least,' said Hack.

Alfie moved uneasily under the stool. Time was passing. The painters might already be on their way.

Fred could be heard calling, 'Hack! Hack! Bother the man. Where is he?'

Hack left hurriedly. Alfie crawled from under the stool and made for the door. Brown turned round. 'Hey, there, Alfie, where are you off to now?'

'Miaow!' cried Alfie, as his tail disappeared round the door. On secret business – and quickly.

Rarely had Alfie's legs covered the distance to the disused station at such speed. Would he be in time to warn Joe before the painters arrived? He found Joe on his knees in the secret garden, while Tansy slept in an old basket nearby. Alfie immediately launched himself on to Joe's back.

'Hey!' cried Joe, taken by surprise. 'Oh, it's only you – what a relief. Back so soon? What's the matter this time?' He laughed as he tried to rise from his knees.

But Alfie clung on to his shoulders and pinned him down. On the alert, the railway cat stiffened suddenly. Joe stayed still and listened, as sounds of a vehicle being

driven slowly down the narrow rutted overgrown lane leading to the back of the station could be heard.

'Help!' muttered Joe. 'We shall have to skedaddle!' Hastily Alfie jumped down and Joe threw garden tools into the bushes, picked up Tansy, basket and all, said, 'Thank you,' to Alfie before disappearing into his secret hiding place in a tangle of bushes in a corner.

Alfie ran round to the front of the station and sat down on the platform. He didn't know what he would do in an emergency, but he was determined to stay around until the danger had passed.

Two painters came on to the platform carrying ladders, paint and brushes. Much to Alfie's surprise Hack followed, holding a long-handled broom and shovel. He stopped in his tracks when he saw Alfie.

'What! *You* here?' was his ungracious greeting. 'Don't I see far too much of you at our own station? Fred's looking everywhere for you. Be off!'

Alfie refused to budge. He spat and hissed as Hack advanced brandishing his broom.

'Leave him alone, Hack!' shouted one of the painters. 'The railway cat's as much right here as anyone. You're always at him.'

Grumbling, Hack started to brush the platform, while the painters set up ladders and began to paint. Hack swept the dust and rubble into a large mound.

Then he looked round to make sure the painters had their backs to him. He was just about to tip the rubbish on to the lines when one of the men turned round.

'Hi! Caught you, Hack!' he cried. 'Stop that dirty habit, or we'll report you.'

'Miaow!' added Alfie, loudly. He often does it that way.

Looking more disgruntled than ever, Hack began to use brush and shovel in the proper manner. When he had finished he lolled about, hands in pockets, looking about him. Suddenly he walked to the edge of the platform and with his back to the track gazed intently at the small waiting room.

Alfie watched him all the time. Why was the man so interested in the place?

Then Hack walked round to the back of the station. Nervously, Alfie followed. Was Hack going to explore the garden? But Hack stood back and surveyed the rear of the building. Then he turned and stared at the tangled garden. His eyes glinted. Alfie moved nearer.

'Mmmm . . .' said Hack out loud. 'Why didn't I think of it before? Marvellous idea. Just large enough and a nice bit of garden. Put it in the wife's name. Make her happy to have a welcome bit of extra money.'

He noticed Alfie. 'Why are you following me round, nuisance?' he said, glaring at the railway cat. 'I'm not telling anyone yet – least of all you – what's in my mind. It's a secret.'

'Miaow!' growled Alfie. Glad to hear your mind's not entirely empty. Don't like the sound of your secret, but I've got a very important secret of my own to think about. Alfie followed Hack to the front of the station, where the men had finished painting.

'Looks almost as clean as my platform,' joked Hack.

*My* platform – what a cheek, thought Alfie. You'd think the man owned the place.

'Want a lift, Alfie?' asked a painter.

'Miaow!' said Alfie. No, thank you. I've got my own affairs to attend to. He turned tail and shot off round to the back of the station and into the undergrowth.

'Always contrary, that cat,' he heard Hack say. 'If it wasn't for Fred spoiling him, I'd train him, I'd . . .'

Alfie hissed. And I'd teach you better manners if only I had the chance!

He waited until the van had been driven off, then he pushed his way into the secret garden. 'Miaow!' he called.

Cautiously, Joe came out of hiding. 'Gone, have they?' he whispered as he put his head on one side and listened. 'I'll have to be more on my guard in future.' He smiled at Alfie. 'I heard them talking and I've learned your name – *Alfie!*'

Alfie stretched out his front paws and scratched furiously at the grass before rolling over on to his back. Joe bent down and pulled his ears. 'Come on, Alfie, show me what these intruders have been up to.'

Alfie led the way to the front of the station and Joe gazed in surprise at the newly-painted building. 'Why do the front only? To impress someone passing by train? Odd – very odd.'

'Miaow!' agreed Alfie. That's just what I think.

Leaving Joe to puzzle over the matter Alfie set off homewards, thankful that all was well with Joe and Tansy – so far . . . Also, he was very hungry.

## 4

# In the Coal-bunker

Alfie was on duty bright and early next morning. The station staff and then the painters soon followed.

'Good start, lads,' said Fred. 'At this rate we'll get everything ready in record time for tomorrow morning.'

'That means *you* keeping out of the way, Alfie,' said Hack rudely.

'Miaow!' said Alfie. And that means *you* getting a move on for once.

The early morning commuters started arriving and as no one else paid them any attention, Alfie greeted each one individually. They talked to him.

'I expect you'll be relieved when things return to normal, Alfie?'

'They've all gone mad – this station will never be the same again.'

'Think I'll take out a bus season-ticket instead of a rail ticket.'

'Miaow!' said Alfie. Please don't do that!

Fred came along holding out a length of blue satin

ribbon. 'I'm going to tie this round Alfie's neck tomorrow,' he announced.

'Huh! Bells on his toes next!' muttered Hack, who was standing nearby.

Fred ignored him. 'Alfie must look handsome for the children's sake,' he said.

'What children?' asked Hack.

'Ah . . .' said Fred mysteriously.

There and then Alfie decided that no one, not even Fred, was going to make him a laughing stock. Blue ribbon, indeed! Fred must be crazy. Alfie stayed around all day and from a safe distance watched the men at work and listened to Fred's frequent outbursts.

'Give this door knob a polish – oil this creaking gate – put some bleach in the water when you swill down the platforms.' Fred went on and on and on.

But, late in the evening, Fred couldn't think of anything more which required attention. Thankfully the painters departed. Fred looked round the station. 'Don't think anyone, even Her Hi . . . er . . . er . . . even anyone could find fault with this station,' he said with pride. He went home leaving Hack in charge of the station for the rest of the evening.

Alfie was resting on a platform seat when Hack crept up on him unawares. 'Ribbon round your neck now?'

he said sarcastically. 'Always wanting to be in the limelight, always needing attention, that's you.'

Alfie opened one eye and looked up at him. Hack went on, 'Well, it wouldn't hurt anyone if you were missing tomorrow morning, would it? Fred would be worried, but it would serve him right for keeping everything a secret.'

Suddenly Hack swooped, grabbed Alfie and carried him off to the rear of the station.

'Miaow! Miaow! Mia . . ow . . . ow . . . .' howled Alfie at the top of his voice. Help! Help! Help! But the station was quiet and deserted. He struggled as Hack, clutching him firmly round the middle, opened the heavy lid of an old coal-bunker and thrust the railway cat into the depths.

'It's only for tonight and tomorrow morning, so make the best of it,' said Hack as he closed the lid.

'Miaow!' cried Alfie. It's cold, dark and dirty in here. Let me out! Let me out! But all he heard was the sound of Hack's retreating footsteps.

Alfie knew the yard was rarely used at night, so in all probability no one would hear him even if he howled his head off. He settled down carefully trying not to disturb the coal dust, but without success. He could feel the black stuff settling all over him.

After what seemed ages – in fact the nearby church

had only struck the hour twice – he heard someone approaching. The lid was raised and moonlight streamed into the bunker.

Joyfully, Alfie prepared to leap out, but a hand restrained him and Hack said, 'I've brought your supper before I sign off duty.' Still holding on to Alfie, he placed a dish on the floor of the bunker.

Alfie glanced in disgust at pieces of minced beef floating in milk. Hack couldn't even take the trouble to use separate dishes! Slovenly, that's what he is, thought Alfie. Tensing himself, he tried to spring out but Hack's grip was too firm.

'Oh, keep still, you stupid cat,' he scolded. 'It's only a joke really. Just to get even with Fred. Eat your supper and be thankful.' He waited. But Alfie couldn't bear the thought of food and refused to eat or drink.

'Turn your nose up at good food, do you?' said Hack. 'All right. I'll take it away.' He reached down, took out the dish and placed it on the ground outside the bunker. He hesitated before shutting the lid and departing, muttering to himself, 'Overfed cat . . .'

Only a joke, thought Alfie? Despicable, that's what he is. Wait until I get out. I'll pay him back somehow. When he had calmed down, he resigned himself to spending the night in such a confined dreary place. As he curled up he felt the gritty coal dust settle into his eyes, his ears and his fur. He shuddered in the darkness. Never had he felt so dirty.

He lay still and quiet as the night dragged on. Then, just after the clock had chimed three, he heard footsteps. Very excited, he was about to start a loud complaining when a thought struck him.

What if the prowler was a criminal, who wouldn't welcome being disturbed by a cat? Or perhaps Hack had relented and had returned to release him? In either case, better wait.

Then, without warning, the lid of the bunker was flung open, a torch shone right into his eyes and a voice he recognized cried, 'Why – it's Alfie! What on earth are you doing down there? Out you come.' In one bound Alfie escaped from his prison.

Joe looked at him in dismay. 'Tut-tut . . . what a sorry sight you are,' he said. 'But, never mind, I'll soon clean you up.'

As he closed the lid he noticed the dish on the ground. 'Food!' he exclaimed. 'Just what I've been searching for. Tansy needs nourishing food to help her recover from her ordeal in the tunnel. I'm sure you won't mind sharing this with her, Alfie?'

'Miaow!' cried Alfie, rubbing against Joe's legs. She can have the lot, and welcome!

Carefully carrying the dish, Joe led the way out of the

station. 'We'll have to take the country lane back to the wayside station,' he told Alfie. 'It's far too dangerous for me to use the embankment. I might be seen and taken into custody for trespassing – and then what would happen to Tansy?'

After his experience in the coal-bunker Alfie thoroughly enjoyed walking in the moonlight with Joe. Once he heard something scuttling in the hedgerow and darted towards the sound. Flat on his stomach he waited on the alert, but nothing moved. After a time he decided there were more important matters to be dealt with and hastened after Joe.

Joe looked down at him and smiled. 'Thought you'd deserted me,' he said.

'Miaow!' said Alfie. Never.

'I'd like to know who shut you up in that ghastly bunker,' Joe said indignantly. 'I'd give him what for!'

'Miaow!' said Alfie again. It's about time somebody put Hack in his place.

They turned down the narrow lane leading to the back of the old station. When they reached the secret garden Joe put the dish on the ground and went to fetch Tansy from the hide-out. When they returned Joe put the kitten down in front of the dish and Alfie watched as she lapped a little milk and nibbled some meat.

'Little and often, that's the menu for a young kitten,'

said Joe as he bent to pick Tansy up. 'Now we're going inside the waiting room for a good sleep,' he said. 'Camp-bed's ready. Coming, Alfie?'

'Miaow!' said Alfie. Yes, please.

Then, 'Miaow!' No, thank you. On second thoughts I'm far too dirty to come inside. I'll have a go at cleaning myself.

Joe waited. 'No? Oh, all right,' he said. 'See you in an hour or so. I'll have to do some very early morning gardening if I am to make more money.' Shining the torch he carried Tansy into the waiting room and closed the door.

Alfie waited until the light went out before he started on himself. It was hard work. His fur was so full of coal dust that no amount of licking made much difference.

Goodness, he thought! This is going to take the rest of the night. Soon the licking became slower and slower and eventually Alfie gave up altogether. He lay down thinking how good it was to relax in the fresh air after being shut up in that horrible coal-bunker.

He had lost all interest in Fred's secret. As for Hack's secret – well, he didn't want to know anything about *that*. He, Alfie, had got his own special secret, which for Joe's sake, no one must ever discover.

Alfie decided he would never, never return to his own station – at least not for a long, long time. He'd definitely stay away until the place was overrun with rats and mice. Then everyone, even Hack, would be overjoyed to see him.

In the meantime he was quite content to be the old disused station's railway cat. He began to feel hungry and as he dozed off he admitted to himself that he would miss tomorrow's liver, which Fred provided once a week.

But, never mind, his secret was more important than food, even if liver was his favourite dish. Or was it? What about the Christmas turkey, or a nice cod steak, or even a plump pork sausage . . . ? Dreaming of food, he fell fast asleep.

## 5

# Very Special Visitors

Alfie woke to find himself surrounded by a thin dawn mist. He got up when he heard a door opening. Joe came out of the waiting room.

'Good morning, my friend!' he said as he bent down and scratched the back of Alfie's head between the ears.

'Prrr . . rrr . . . rr . . . .' sang Alfie. I like that – do it again!

Playfully Joe ruffled his fur and a cloud of coal dust rose into the air. 'Phew! You do look a mess,' laughed Joe. 'But don't worry. First, digging – then, before I go off with my barrow-load of vegetables, I'll get busy on you with sponge, brush and comb. You'll look as good as new.'

'Tansy's still asleep,' Joe went on. 'I'll share the food between you later. Amuse yourself for a little while.'

'Miaow!' said Alfie. Certainly.

He went round to the front of the station and sat down on the platform. Soon a train passed on the Up line. The driver waved. Not long afterwards a freight train trundled through the station. The driver saluted.

Very satisfactory, thought Alfie. He always enjoyed being recognized by his fellow railway workers.

Time passed and there was no sign of Joe or Tansy. Might as well have another go at cleaning myself while I'm waiting, decided Alfie. He hoped Joe wouldn't go on digging all morning as he was beginning to feel really hungry.

Alfie spread out the toes of his right forepaw intending to lick them clean, when he heard another train approaching from the London direction. With his tongue hanging out he watched the train, puzzled, for it was slowing down.

Good gracious – it's going to stop *here*, thought Alfie! How strange. It must be a ghost train. Or perhaps it had something to do with Fred's secret? Was it a special train? It didn't look special. He waited fascinated as the two-coach diesel drew up at the platform.

A door opened and out stepped a boy and a girl, followed by a lady. A door further down the train burst open at the same time and an attendant rushed forward. 'Excuse me, ma'am,' he gasped. 'The driver has made a mistake. This is the wrong station. We are expected at the *next* one.' He beckoned to the children to get back into the train.

'But I want to stay and see over this little station,' cried the girl. 'It looks gorgeous.'

'Yes, just the kind of station we wanted to visit,' said the boy as he peered through a chink in the window-boards. 'There's a waiting room and a booking office!'

'And there's a CAT,' shouted the girl as she caught sight of Alfie. 'He's very dirty but he's got lovely greeny-yellow eyes and he looks friendly.'

The children rushed up to Alfie, who arched his back and purred a welcome as they stroked and petted him.

The attendant was very worried. 'Please, ma'am,' he said. 'We're already ten minutes late for our appointment.'

The lady looked at the children and smiled. 'They really are enjoying themselves, Thompson,' she said. 'We'll let them stay for just a few minutes.'

Without warning, Joe, carrying Tansy, appeared round a corner of the waiting room. He halted in astonishment when he saw the group on the platform. 'Good heavens – royalty – a princess!' he muttered as he turned to flee.

But the princess put up a hand and called out, 'Wait a minute, please.'

The children ran up to Joe. 'There's a kitten as well,' cried the girl. 'Poor little thing, it's injured.'

'Tansy will soon be well again,' Joe assured her. He was very embarrassed at being the centre of attention.

'Tansy – what a lovely name,' said the princess as she

shook hands with Joe. 'We are supposed to be at the next station on a very private visit,' she told him. 'The children are interested in railways and wanted to be shown round a station as other children are.'

While the children, and Alfie, rushed about examining everything, the princess talked to Joe, and when he had overcome his shyness, he told her about being out of work.

Thompson joined them. 'Please, ma'am,' he said again. 'We must be holding up other trains on the line.'

'Oh, dear, I am sorry,' she said. 'We'd better hurry. Come children –' But the children, and Alfie, had disappeared.

'They must have gone round to the back, ma'am,' said Joe.

'Well, we'd better go and find them, quickly,' said the princess.

At the rear of the waiting room, the princess gazed in surprise at the peeling paintwork and broken window. 'What one might call "putting a good front on it"!' she said with a twinkle in her eyes.

The children could not be seen, but shouts were heard and Joe said, 'I know where they are,' as he parted the bushes for the princess to go through.

They found the children, and Alfie, in the secret garden chasing about all over the place. Alfie stopped to dig his claws into the bark of a tree, pulling them in and out, in and out in his excitement.

'I'm sure this is the very best station in the whole world,' shouted the boy.

'And this is a *secret* garden!' added the girl.

'I can see that,' said the princess smiling. She turned to Joe. 'Is this your garden?'

Joe hung his head. 'Well, not really, ma'am,' he admitted. 'I use it – without permission – to grow vegetables for sale. It's my livelihood.' He hesitated. 'We – Tansy and me, that is – we'll have to go now I've been found out.'

The princess looked sympathetic. 'Well, we'll see . . .' she said as she glanced round. 'It's a very well-kept little garden. You're going to have a good healthy crop of vegetables.'

She turned to the children. 'No nonsense, now,' she said firmly. 'We really must be on our way.'

'Oh, no – *please*. We're enjoying ourselves,' they cried.'

'Miaow!' cried Alfie. Me too!

Suddenly Alfie rushed into the bushes. Before the princess could stop them the children followed, pushing through shrubs which pricked them and tore their clothes. They came to Joe's hide-out in a corner and with shrieks of excitement they examined the

camp-bed, the first aid box and Joe's bits and pieces, which were all he possessed in the world.

'We could hide here for weeks and weeks,' shouted the boy.

'For months and months,' echoed the girl.

'Prrr . . rrr . . . rrr . . . .' said Alfie. For ever perhaps!

But the princess was calling, 'Children, children – *we must be going*!'

And Joe shouted as he pushed his way through the bushes, 'I'll bring them back.' Soon, laughing and shouting, the children returned to the waiting princess.

She put a hand to her lips when she saw them. 'Oh!' she exclaimed. '*Oh!* Look at your clothes – and your hair – and your faces and . . . Well, you'll have to come along as you are. There's no time left to clean you up. We've kept our hosts waiting long enough as it is.' Reluctantly the children followed her.

'Look after Tansy,' the princess called to Joe. She glanced at Alfie. 'And soap and water wouldn't come amiss on him.' She laughed. 'But it isn't every day we find a cat and a kitten – and a nice grown-up – in a secret garden.'

Joe, with Tansy, and Alfie followed the group back to the platform. As the princess led the way into the train she said, 'Here we go on our way to the real station.'

That's *my* station, thought Alfie proudly. He felt sorry he wouldn't be on duty to greet the royal party. Whatever would Fred say if he saw him covered in coal dust? But wasn't it part of the railway cat's duties to be in attendance for special occasions? And wasn't this a very special occasion?

Alfie looked up at Joe, who nodded. The railway cat made up his mind. In one bound, just as the door was closing, he leapt into the train. Scampering down the gangway he jumped on to the seat occupied by the royal children, who immediately hugged him. Clouds of black dust covered all three.

The princess looked on in dismay. 'Oh, dear,' she said in a flurry. 'I'll have to try and do something about you.' She glanced out of the window. 'Oh, *dear*,' she said again, helplessly. 'The train's slowing down. There isn't time!'

'Miaow!' cried Alfie, very excited. True. There isn't time. We're nearly there and some people are in for a very big surprise . . .

# 6

# Good News

Everything looks very smart, thought Alfie, as the train drew into his station. His eyes widened when he saw Fred, Hack, Brown and the rest of the staff lined up each side of a strip of red carpet, which had been laid on the platform. A flower arrangement on a tall pedestal looked very decorative. Trust Fred to do the job properly!

The train stopped. Alfie leapt off the seat and was first at the door. It was opened from the outside and as the staff waited expectantly for the royal party to alight – out stepped a very dirty cat!

Fred cried, 'Oh, *no*!' before clapping a hand to his mouth, while Hack muttered, 'Blimey – trust Alfie!' The staff stared in disbelief at the unkempt railway cat and the two royal children, their faces and clothes smeared with coal dust.

With head held high and the tip of his tail waving, Alfie led the little procession along the carpet. When the princess stopped to speak to a member of staff, Alfie stopped. When she continued walking, Alfie did the same. Once he was compelled to sit down and have a really good scratch with his left hind leg. Black coal dust settled on the red carpet as he did so.

Fred hissed, 'Stop that, Alfie!'

'But what is he supposed to do when he itches?' asked the boy.

'Coal dust is such irritating stuff,' said the princess. 'I must apologize for my children's appearance today.'

The morning passed very quickly as Fred conducted the royal party on a tour of the station. Alfie went along as well, although twice Fred tried to wave him away and Hack said from the corner of his mouth, 'Disgusting behaviour!'

The children were very polite and interested in everything. When the visit came to an end and everybody had been thanked, the boy said, 'We like this station very much, but the little one up the line *is* rather special.'

'Yes – with Joe and the kitten and the secret garden,' added the girl.

'Joe? Kitten? Secret garden?' said Fred, puzzled. He turned to the princess. 'I don't understand what they mean, ma'am.'

So she told him about Joe and Tansy and the garden.

'Well, of all the cheek,' muttered Hack. 'A man making use of my . . .' He stopped and looked round furtively.

The children said an affectionate farewell to Alfie before they boarded the train for the homeward journey. 'He's the most intelligent cat we've ever met,' said the boy.

Alfie glanced sideways at Hack. Then he sat on the platform with paws together and tail neatly tucked in as the train departed, with the children and their mother waving from a window.

After all the excitement Alfie felt rather tired and was making his way towards the staff room, with the easy chair in mind, when Fred caught up with him.

'Oh, no, you don't, Alfie!' he cried. 'Not until I've cleaned you up – and how you need it.'

'He's an absolute disgrace to the railway, that cat,' said Hack. 'Dirty, unreliable and I'm sure it was his fault the royal party was late . . .'

'Oh, shut up, Hack!' cried Fred, exasperated. He picked Alfie up and took him along to a quiet corner of the platform. And there, for the first time in his life, Alfie actually *enjoyed* a very good wash and brush-up.

Afterwards Alfie had his first meal of the day – liver, his favourite food, which in spite of all the goings-on

Fred had remembered to bring for him. Good old Fred. Alfie sighed with contentment.

Things settled down again after the royal visit. Of course, Alfie's secret was now common knowledge. Everyone knew about Joe but, so far, no one had ordered him off the old station.

'It's a matter for Headquarters to decide,' said Fred, when anyone raised the question as to whether Joe should be told to leave or not. 'Joe is trespassing, but he's really a very honest, industrious person and you never know . . .'

But Alfie was worried. He often walked along the embankment to visit Joe and Tansy. Occasionally Fred went as well, taking with him a loaf of bread or some home-made cakes for Joe and liver or lights, or perhaps a cod's head, for the kitten.

To everyone's surprise Hack often went to the old station, where he would glance round in a secretive manner. He was always irritated when he met Alfie there.

'Can't have *you* lurking about here,' he would say.

'Miaow!' Alfie would hiss. What's it got to do with you where I am? You and your silly secret.

One day when Alfie arrived at the wayside station he found Fred and Hack talking to Joe. Hack was very annoyed when he saw Alfie.

'You here again – always poking your nose into other people's affairs,' he shouted. 'Wish I'd locked you in that coal-bunker for good.'

'What!' yelled Fred, red in the face. 'You mean to say *you* did that to Alfie? Our Alfie, the friendliest and most efficient cat we've ever had?'

Alfie rolled over and over gleefully.

'You scoundrel!' cried Joe, his eyes flashing. 'I'd like to shut you up in that coal-bunker for a whole month without food or drink.'

'And it would give me great pleasure to send you down a coal-mine for good,' added Fred. He glared at Hack, who went crimson, shuffled his feet and looked ashamed.

'It was only a joke really,' he murmured.

'Joke!' cried Fred and Joe in unison, while Alfie growled, 'Brrr . . brrr . . . brrr. . . .'

'What have you got against Alfie? Why shouldn't he come here as often as he likes?' said Fred. 'And if it comes to that, why do you haunt the place?'

'Yes, tell us that,' put in Joe. 'You're always prowling round, watching me.'

Hack glanced up and down the line, looked at his watch and announced, 'Well, it's time for me to report for duty. I'll be off.' He started to walk away.

'Not before you've given us an answer,' said Fred, blocking his path.

'And a true one,' said Joe.

'Well, er . . . as a matter of fact,' began Hack. 'Er . . . well, it's no business of yours!'

'Oh, yes, it is,' said Fred firmly.

'But it's a secret,' shouted Hack.

'Let us into the secret then,' said Fred, as he stared hard at Hack.

'Oh, well, I suppose you'll all have to know sooner or later,' he said. 'I've made an offer to buy this little station for my wife. She intends making it into a holiday cottage and renting it to people in the summer to make some extra money for us.'

Alfie couldn't believe his ears. A holiday cottage? What about Joe and the garden – and Tansy? Very worried, he looked up at Fred, who for the moment was dumbstruck, while Joe was filled with dismay. Fred was the first to pull himself together. He patted Joe on the shoulder.

'Don't worry, Joe,' he said. 'His offer hasn't been accepted yet.'

'Oh, but I'm sure it's in the bag,' boasted Hack. 'I expect an acceptance of my offer by post tomorrow morning.'

And next morning's post did bring a reply for Hack –

but it wasn't what he had hoped for. He brought the letter to show Fred. 'They won't let me buy the old station,' he raged.

Fred said nothing.

'And it's that cat's fault – making up to royalty as he did,' Hack went on.

'It's got nothing to do with Alfie,' said Fred. 'Come on, Hack, trains won't wait while we stand here talking.'

Next day Joe came along to Alfie's station. He also had received a letter, which he handed to Fred to read. The smile on Fred's face broadened as his eyes scanned the page.

'Why, Joe, this is good news,' he cried. 'You're to be a tenant of the old station. Hear that, Alfie? And the building is to be modernized and made into a small dwelling.'

'Prrr . . rrrr . . . rrrr. . . .' said Alfie. Best bit of news I've ever heard.

Hack came along. 'Listen to this, Hack,' said Fred. He read the letter out loud.

'Oh!' said Hack when Fred had finished. He looked down at the platform and shuffled his feet. Then he drew himself up, went across and shook hands with Joe. 'Congratulations, Joe,' he said. 'I'm sure you need the station and garden more than I do.'

'Miaow!' cried Alfie, astonished. Well, I never! But that's the spirit. One day I might *possibly* understand Hack.

Alfie jumped up at Joe, then with the tip of his tail waving, raced along the platform, leapt on and off seats, trucks and mail bags, before running over the bridge and back again to the group.

'Well done, Alfie,' laughed Fred. 'Now back to work everyone.'

Alfie kept a watchful eye on developments at Joe's station. Very soon the waiting room became a living room, the ticket office a bedroom, and a small bathroom was built on at the back.

In between gardening and selling the produce, Joe painted the back of the building, weeded between the platform slabs, mended the fence and gate, put a new brass knocker on the front door and dug up the uncultivated part of the garden. Eventually everything was completed and the wayside station was declared open for the sale of fruit and vegetables.

Joe worked harder than ever. Alfie wished he could urge all passengers to go along and buy his fruit and vegetables. He need not have worried, for Fred – and to Alfie's surprise Hack also – distributed leaflets to passengers and villagers giving information about Joe's new nursery garden.

## Good News

And everyone was happy – everyone that is, except Hack, who often looked very *unhappy*. Alfie felt sorry about this for he didn't like anyone to be miserable.

Could anything be done to help Hack?

# 7

# The Old Railway Carriage

Day by day Alfie watched Hack as the man shuffled along the platforms and answered passengers' questions in a surly manner. Whatever *could* one do to help such a miserable man, thought Alfie? One day he overheard Fred taking Hack to task about his shortcomings.

'The fact is, I'm worn out,' said Hack. 'The wife keeps on and on and on about missing the chance to buy the little station – as though it was my fault.' He glared at Alfie. 'That cat has a lot to answer for.'

'Nonsense!' said Fred shortly. 'I'm sorry you are worried but passengers have been complaining about your manners and I won't have that while I'm in charge of the station.'

Stern words from Fred, thought Alfie.

Hack was silent as he looked down at the floor. 'Well, I'll just have to try harder to be pleasant,' he said at last.

One day Alfie decided to go for a walk through the surrounding fields, as a change from his station work. He gambolled about in the long grass enjoying the spring sunshine and chasing everything that moved. At the end of a small field he came across a shed. At least, at first glance, it looked like a shed, but on closer inspection it turned out to be an old railway carriage.

Alfie walked round the carriage until he came to a door. He pushed it open and entered the carriage. The door closed behind him. He looked round with interest. The place was bare, but there was evidence that the farmer had recently used the carriage as a large chicken coop. Feathers lay about the floor.

Alfie nosed round. No mice. What a pity. Nothing left for them to nibble now the chicken feed had disappeared, he supposed. Rays from the setting sun shone through the grimy window panes. Time to go, he thought. He made for the door, forgetting it had closed behind him. There was no other exit.

Trapped again! Was it his lot in life to be shut up in undesirable places, thought Alfie? All he could do was sit down on the dusty floor and wait patiently in the hope that someone would come along and let him out.

He listened to birds singing, and to the pitter-patter of their feet on the carriage roof. Small creatures scuttled round and under the carriage. By the end of the second day of his captivity he was sure he wouldn't be able to last much longer without food and drink. Never had he felt so frustrated.

Next morning, however, he heard sounds in the

distance. He pricked up his ears. The sounds came nearer. Then Alfie got up and rushed to the door excitedly, for he recognized Hack's voice calling.

'Digby! Heel, I say – come back!'

'Woof! Woof! Woof!' barked a dog.

Alfie guessed that Hack was taking his dog, Digby, for a walk through the fields and that Digby had sensed his, Alfie's, presence in the carriage. Alfie's miaowing and banging against the door became more frenzied. He couldn't bear the thought of Hack catching Digby and leading him away without coming into the carriage. But, to his relief, Alfie heard Digby barking as he jumped up the door.

'Woof! Woof! Woof!' howled Digby.

'Miaow! Miaow! Miaow!' cried Alfie.

'Caught you!' cried Hack and Alfie heard the man fastening the lead on to Digby's collar. 'I'll tie you to this hook for a time – teach you to obey orders.'

Alfie fell back as the door opened. Hack entered and closed the door behind him. He stared in surprise when he saw Alfie. 'Well, well, Alfie, you're a right one for getting locked in, aren't you?' he said as he gave Alfie a friendly pat. 'You must have been here for two or three days. Hungry, I expect? Fred's been out the last two nights looking for you.'

Hands in pockets, Hack gazed round the carriage.

'Hmmm . . . it's a more cheerful place than the coal-bunker,' he said. 'But that was only for a few hours.'

'Miaow!' wailed Alfie. I've forgotten about the coal-bunker, but let me out, please. I *am* hungry!

Hack hadn't finished his inspection. Slowly he paced the length and breadth of the carriage. Then he stood right in the middle and stared ahead, deep in thought. Suddenly he snapped his fingers and cried, 'The very thing! Back to the station, Alfie, I've got some business to do.' He flung the door wide open.

Alfie didn't wait for a skirmish with Digby. Off he sped back to the station and Fred.

Fred was so pleased to see him that he forgot to scold. Instead he rushed into the staff room and prepared Alfie's first meal for three days – a dish of fish and a saucer of cream. Cream! Almost worth the discomfort of being locked up, thought Alfie, as he started on his meal.

Soon Hack arrived. The man was panting with the effort of controlling Digby on the lead. Digby surged forward when he saw Alfie but Hack pulled him back and ordered him to sit down.

Fred looked up surprised. 'Hello!' he said. 'What's brought you here before duty time?'

Hack could hardly get the words out. 'Fo . . . found Alfie in that old carriage by the stream in Farmer Lunt's field,' he gasped. 'Had a . . . a . . . a brilliant idea. With a few alterations that old carriage could be made into an ideal holiday cottage – in open country, not far from the station.'

Hack sighed. 'If only Lunt would let me buy it.'

'Well . . . there's a chance he might,' said Fred thoughtfully. 'I heard a few weeks ago that he was prepared to sell the carriage, and a patch of ground, if a suitable offer came along.'

'Really?' shouted Hack, his eyes shining.

Fred nodded. 'But don't forget,' he said, 'you might never have known about the carriage if Alfie hadn't been shut in and if Digby hadn't led you to him.' Fred winked at Alfie. 'Excellent cat, our Alfie!'

'Er . . . yes . . . er, yes, he is,' said Hack, with a lopsided grin at Alfie. 'Sometimes!' he added. He and Digby set off homewords.

And in due time the old railway carriage became a holiday cottage. Hack, assisted at times by Fred and Joe – and hindered by Alfie getting in the way – worked hard on the carriage making it comfortable for visitors. But it would never, never look as attractive as Joe's wayside station, Alfie decided.

Hack was a changed man. When on duty he was helpful and courteous to passengers, and occasionally he stopped to stroke Alfie and have a word with him.

'Wonders will never cease!' marvelled Fred.

Alfie was pleased, but he wasn't going to accept too much attention from Hack. He didn't think the man would ever really like cats. However, for the time being, Alfie was content to be friends.

The station settled down into its ordinary routine until one day Fred made an announcement. 'The royal train – the *real* royal train – will be passing through the station next Tuesday.' He grinned at Alfie. 'I understand some of the royal children will be on board. Think you'll get a wave, Alfie?'

'Miaow!' cried Alfie. Sure I will.

When Tuesday came, Alfie was in a dilemma. Should he stay at his own station, or should he go along to Joe's wayside station to be with his two friends when the royal train went past?

He decided that Fred could manage without him, so off he went along the now familiar route. Tansy, completely recovered, waited quietly beside Joe as Alfie, unable to control his excitement, dashed up and down the platform and round and round the garden.

'Calm down!' laughed Joe.

And soon, 'Here it comes!' he shouted as he stood to attention, white handkerchief at the ready to wave.

The bright, gleaming royal train (not a two-coach diesel this time) slackened speed as it approached the

wayside station. Was it going to stop here, thought Alfie? The train didn't halt but it slowed down so that two children – two clean and tidy children – could lean out of a window and wave vigorously at the man, cat and kitten on the platform.

Joe waved back, Tansy rolled over on to her side while Alfie rushed to the end of the platform alongside the train as it gathered speed. Joe called him back in case, in his enthusiasm, the railway cat followed the royal train into the tunnel!

Alfie stayed for a time and watched Joe at work. Customers now came from far and near to buy his fruit and vegetables, which were the best Alfie had ever seen. He thought he had never seen anyone work as hard as Joe.

Although Joe was such a busy man, he never forgot to grow plenty of catmint for his friend Alfie, the railway cat. And Alfie often visited the wayside station to play with Tansy in the garden, which was no longer a secret garden, but one which had received *royal* approval . . .

# The Railway Cat
## and the Horse

# Contents

# 1

# An Important Consignment

Mustn't miss anything, thought Alfie the railway cat, as he ran towards a group of station staff assembled on platform No. 2.

'Ah, good. All present now you're here, Alfie,' said Fred, the Chargeman, who was Alfie's special friend. 'Listening, everyone? I'm expecting an important consignment from the west country later today. Extra care will be required in unloading.'

'Aren't we busy enough as it is?' grumbled Leading Railman Hack. 'We should be paid extra for dealing with awkward jobs.'

Really! One never knew how that man was going to behave, thought Alfie. One minute complaining, next minute nice as pie.

'Tell us what it is, Fred,' said Brown, the Booking Clerk.

'Well . . . er . . . it's . . . er . . . it's . . .' mumbled Fred.

'Out with it,' said Hack impatiently.

'It's a horse,' said Fred smiling.

'A *horse*!' repeated Hack. 'But horses are not conveyed by rail nowadays.'

'Er . . . not usually,' said Fred, 'but this is rather special.'

'Probably a racehorse on its way to the Mead training stables,' said Brown. 'It might be valuable.'

'Do you think so?' said Hack excitedly.

'It's certainly worth a lot of money,' said Fred still smiling. (Alfie noticed that his eyes were twinkling.)

Hack rubbed his hands together. 'I've always been a good judge of horses,' he said. 'It will be interesting to take a close look at this one.'

'What's its name?' asked Brown.

'Rex,' said Fred, with a hand to his mouth.

There was a buzz of excitement about the station all morning. 'We're waiting for delivery of a very fine horse,' said Hack to one passenger after another.

But the railway cat was puzzled as, from time to time, he caught sight of the amused expression on Fred's face – a sure sign that his friend had something up his sleeve!

Shortly after midday the staff, including Alfie, assembled on the Up platform.

'Here she comes!' shouted Hack as the train approached.

Waving his tail, Alfie rushed up and down the platform. The guard poked his head out and shouted, 'Hello, Alfie!'

'Miaow!' sang Alfie.

Hack moved forward.

'Hold on a minute, Hack,' said Fred. 'We are about to handle a very superior horse. Great care must be taken.'

'Hope he doesn't bite,' said Brown.

Fred laughed as he shook his head. Hack's eyes scanned the length of the train as it drew up at the platform. 'There's no horse vehicle on this train,' he cried as he glanced accusingly at Fred.

'Er, no . . .' said Fred. He walked forward as the door of the guard's van was opened from inside. 'He's in here.'

'In the *guard's* van?' shouted Hack. 'Have you gone clean off your head?'

Alfie followed Fred into the van. 'Miaow!' he greeted the guard.

'Hello, Alfie,' said the guard. 'Come to meet Rex?'

'Miaow!' cried Alfie.

'Where is he?' demanded Hack as he leapt into the van. He took a quick look round and turned to Fred. 'Where is this wonder horse?' he sneered, his face red with annoyance. 'I believe you've been pulling my leg. There's no horse.'

'Oh, yes, there is,' said Fred. 'Calm down. We've got a job to do.'

Alfie followed Fred to a large wooden crate in a corner of the van. 'He's in here,' said Fred.

There was silence for a moment and Hack's eyes widened in disbelief. Alfie peered through a chink in the crate and, sure enough, saw part of a hoof and a foreleg. *But* – they were not flesh and blood limbs!

Alfie looked up at Fred. 'Miaow!' he cried. It's very naughty of you to tease Hack.

230

'Come off it, Fred,' cried Hack. 'Admit it, there's no horse.'

'But there is,' insisted Fred. 'I never said it was a racehorse. It's an old rocking-horse, which aroused interest when it appeared in a television series recently.'

For once Hack was dumbfounded, while Alfie rolled over and over at Fred's feet. Of course, he should have guessed! Only this morning he had overheard Fred talking on the telephone to old Mr Brock, the rocking-horse mender.

'Come on, everyone, lend a hand,' ordered Fred. 'The van's waiting outside to take Rex to Mr Brock's. By rights we should have a security guard with us.'

'You're kidding!' cried Hack.

'No, seriously,' said Fred. 'No one knows Rex's age, but he has been owned by several generations of the same family and there's a lot of interest in old rocking-horses at present.'

'No interest to me,' said Hack sourly. Reluctantly he moved forward to help unload.

Alfie decided he would be first at Mr Brock's to welcome Rex. Off he ran and covered the half mile to the workshop in record time. As he trotted down the passage at the side of the house, where Mr Brock lived alone, he breathed in a lovely familiar mixed-up smell of

231

leather soap, polish, oil and paint coming from the workshop at the end of the passage.

Alfie halted in the open doorway. Brush in hand, the rocking-horse mender stood in the middle of the workshop putting a coat of paint on a large rocking-horse. Around him were rocking-horses of all sizes, some on rockers, others on swingers.

Some of the horses were waiting to be repainted, some had saddle or harness missing, while others were short of an eye, an ear, a tail or a mane. Many of them were like old friends to Alfie as they had been in the workshop for a long time. The railway cat was a regular visitor at Mr Brock's.

The old man looked up. 'Hello, Alfie!' he cried. 'I'm glad to see you. Taking a rest from station duties?'

'Miaow!' said Alfie as, purring loudly, he leapt forward and rubbed against Mr Brock's legs.

There was the sound of a vehicle braking outside. Hurriedly Mr Brock put down his brush. 'Ah, good!' he exclaimed as he made for the door. 'That must be Rex. This is going to be the most interesting restoration job I have ever undertaken.'

Very excited, Alfie followed him back down the passage and into the road, where Fred and Hack were helping the van driver manoeuvre the crate out of the van and on to a trolley.

Mr Brock dithered about, got in the way and issued advice, until Fred patted his shoulder and said kindly, 'Leave it to us, Mr Brock.'

The passage was just wide enough to take the trolley. 'There's really no need for three of us to move this thing,' protested Hack. He stumbled across Alfie and scraped the crate against the wall.

'It's that cat's fault,' he yelled. 'Makes my blood boil the way he belts about like a rocket.'

'Oh, dear! Oh, dear!' moaned Mr Brock. 'Do be careful, please, Hack. Rex must come to no harm. In my opinion he could be very valuable and I'm nervous of having him in my charge.'

The rocking-horse mender ran ahead into the work-shop and moved some of the horses to make a space for Rex. The crate was wheeled inside. It was soon opened and the rocking-horse was revealed. Everyone stared, for Rex was a sorry sight. Two hundred years' wear and tear showed only too plainly. The horse's legs, which were stretched at full gallop, were damaged. There was a faded red saddle on his back and the tattered remains of a leather bridle hung from his jaws.

A few strands of gingery hair were all that remained of the mane and tail. The body was a dull grey with brown splotches here and there, relieved only by a white diamond on the forehead. No matter, thought

Alfie. He knew that with great skill and patience Mr Brock would turn Rex into a beautiful creature again.

But, 'Huh! Call that thing valuable?' jeered Hack. 'I've seen better articles in a junk shop.'

'Brrr . . . rr . . . rr . . .' growled Alfie. Rude man, Hack.

'You'll have to eat your words when Mr Brock has finished working on Rex,' said Fred.

The rocking-horse mender smiled and nodded as he gently stroked the horse and moved him to and fro on the long rockers. 'Many children have enjoyed riding Rex,' he murmured. 'Now, sadly, Mr Stanley, his present owner, is forced to sell him, along with other family heirlooms.'

'But why?' asked Fred.

'To raise enough money to repair the family's old mansion, otherwise that too will have to be sold,' sighed Mr Brock.

'What a pity,' said Fred. 'Cheer up, Mr Brock. Hack and I will have to go back to work, but I'll leave Alfie with you, if you wish.'

'Oh, thank you, Fred,' said the old man. 'I'm always pleased to have Alfie's company when you can spare him.'

'We can *always* spare . . .' began Hack.

'Now then, Hack,' Fred interrupted. 'Just give a hand with the crate.'

They both moved the crate into a corner before leaving Mr Brock's workshop.

'Prrr . . . rr . . . rr . . . rrr. . .' sang Alfie happily. It was lunch-time and he was always sure of a titbit or two from his old friend, the rocking-horse mender, who was particularly good with a lean bacon and cheese fry.

# 2

# Alfie is Worried

On his return to the station Alfie found an ill-tempered Hack in charge. As he didn't want the station to get a bad name the railway cat made himself very pleasant to passengers. During the afternoon a smartly dressed man stepped from a London train. He bent down and tickled Alfie under the chin.

'Miaow!' said Alfie as he flopped on to his back and rolled his head, inviting more attention.

Hack came along. 'Always sucking up to people, that cat,' he said scornfully.

The man glanced up. 'Please direct me to the rocking-horse mender's workshop,' he said.

'And what do *you* want with Mr Brock?' asked Hack suspiciously.

'That's none of your business,' was the firm reply.

'Oh, yes it is!' retorted Hack. 'There's a valuable hor . . .' He stopped short. 'Anyhow, *I'm* boss here until Fred comes back, and I'm telling you nothing.'

'And *I'm* a senior Government official on private business,' said the man glaring at Hack.

'Ho! Ho! Expect me to believe that,' shouted Hack. 'I've heard of your sort. You're up to no good, I'm sure of that.'

At that moment Fred came running down the stairs. 'Sir!' he gasped. 'I'm sorry, but I've only just received a message about your visit.'

Hack went red in the face and put a hand to his mouth. Fred glanced from one to the other. 'Is anything wrong?' he asked.

'There is,' said the Government official. 'I asked this man a civil question and received a very rude response. He must be reported for insolence. But in the meantime please tell me the way to the rocking-horse mender's workshop.'

'Certainly, sir,' said Fred as he led the way to the front of the station.

'I was only trying to protect the old horse,' said Hack furiously to no one in particular.

'Miaow!' said Alfie quietly. I know you were. When Fred came back he was very annoyed and gave Hack a good ticking off. 'Just show better judgement in future,' he advised, 'and don't dare be rude to *any* passenger.'

Hack stuck his hands in his pockets and kicked at a platform seat.

'Stop that!' shouted Fred.

'I was only thinking of Rex,' said Hack. 'That man might not be genuine.'

'Nonsense!' said Fred. 'He's what he said he is, a senior Government official. Stop playing at being a detective and get on with your real duties.'

Hack went about all day looking very aggrieved. Alfie felt sorry for him. Anyone could make a mistake, couldn't they? When later in the day the official returned to the station to catch a London train, Alfie made him very welcome. Hack hovered about nearby and when the train arrived at the platform he rushed forward and opened a door for the man. 'I'm sorry I was uncivil, sir,' he said.

'That's all right, forget it this time,' said the man. 'But watch your step in future.'

That night Alfie, unable to sleep, moved restlessly in his basket. He was worried. If Rex was really valuable would someone try to steal him in the middle of the night while Mr Brock slept in his house?

Eventually Alfie gave up trying to settle down. He left the waiting room by climbing through a ventilator in the window and made his way to Mr Brock's. He crept down the passage at the side of the house, stopping now and then to listen. The only sound was an owl hooting in a nearby copse. Silently Alfie leapt on to a window sill and gazed into the workshop.

239

Having very good eyesight and helped by light from the moon, he could just make out Rex's shadowy form surrounded by the other rocking-horses. Alfie stayed for a while, listening and looking. It was very quiet. Satisfied that all was well, he was about to jump down when, from inside the workshop, he heard a sort of grunting noise. He peered through the window and saw something moving on the floor near Rex.

Alfie's fears were justified – BURGLARS, he thought! Flustered, he looked round for a possible entrance into the workshop and noticed a small ventilator in the window. He was used to ventilators so, with no great effort, he stretched up and slipped into the workshop.

Ears back and tail quivering, he moved very very slowly across the floor towards Rex. With tensed muscles, he crouched down before springing at a figure on the floor alongside the old horse.

There was a yell and a scream as Alfie landed right on top of someone lying on a camp-bed. The bed collapsed and Alfie found himself on the floor by a man.

'Oh! Oh! Oh!' shrieked the man, and what a surprise Alfie had, for the voice was *Mr Brock's*! The old man lashed out and hit Alfie on the nose.

'Mia . . . ow . . . ow . . .' moaned Alfie as he lay sprawled on the floor. It's only me!

'Oh, dear, is that you, Alfie?' gasped Mr Brock as he

241

put out a hand to calm the railway cat. 'You did give me a terrible fright. My heart's beating like a hammer. I'll have to lie quiet for a while.'

Alfie stretched out beside his friend and purred encouragingly. It took at least half an hour for Mr Brock to recover from the shock. At last he managed to laugh. 'Really, Alfie!' he cried. 'Here am I doing my best to guard Rex night and day, and I am attacked by one of my very good friends.'

'Miaow!' said Alfie. I'm sorry.

'Never mind,' said Mr Brock. He shook off the rumpled blankets covering him and got to his feet. 'I'm sure you didn't mean to frighten me.' He switched on the light and looked down at the camp-bed, flat on the floor. 'I'll have to get this bed to rights first.'

Alfie watched as the old man struggled to put the bed and blankets into position again. When this had been done Mr Brock stood back panting. 'Now, Alfie,' he said, 'shall we have a drink together before we try to get some sleep?'

Mr Brock picked up a thermos flask from a table and poured some milky coffee into a saucer, which he put on the floor. 'There you are, Alfie,' he said.

Alfie waited politely. 'Now one for me,' said Mr Brock as he filled a cup from the flask. 'Cheers, Alfie!' he said as he raised the cup.

'Miaow!' said Alfie. He put down his head and lapped noisily. He was very fond of milky coffee.

Mr Brock switched off the light and got back into bed. 'Come on, Alfie,' he said. 'There's room for you.'

Alfie wasted no time in accepting the invitation by leaping on to the bed. 'Careful!' cried Mr Brock in alarm. 'You'll have us both on the floor again.'

Alfie kneaded the top blanket with his paws and followed his tail in a circle several times before he settled down with a flop in the curve of Mr Brock's legs.

'I'll be unable to move for the rest of the night,' laughed Mr Brock, 'but you'll keep me nice and warm, Alfie.'

They were quiet for a time, then Mr Brock started to talk to himself, and to Alfie. 'Had a Government man in this morning. He wanted to know all about Rex, where he came from, when he was going to be sold, etc. The man is eager to buy Rex for his private antique collection but, regretfully, I had to tell him I'm certain he would be outbid at auction.'

The old man sighed as he pulled the bedclothes over his shoulders and nearly dislodged Alfie. 'Such a pity,' he said. 'I'm so afraid a foreigner will make the highest bid and Rex will be taken out of this country.'

Mr Brock's eyes closed and he started to wheeze and then to snore softly. Before Alfie drifted off to sleep he

gazed round at the horses. They looked so alert, almost alive, in the moonlight that Alfie imagined they might all gallop off along a moonbeam. Silly, he told himself! The railway cat's eyes closed and he dreamed he was rocking, rocking, rocking.

Mr Brock was an early riser. 'I'll just go along to the house for a wash and brush-up and breakfast, before I start work on Rex,' he said. 'I've put a little minced beef aside for you, so come along, Alfie.'

Back in the workshop after breakfast Alfie watched Mr Brock at work on Rex. First the faded red saddle and leather bridle were removed, then the straggly mane and tail were cut off.

'I'll have to strip off all the old paint first,' said the rocking-horse mender. 'The ears need mending and the legs strengthening. Believe me, there's a great deal of work to be done before Rex is restored to my satisfaction.'

After a while Mr Brock looked at his watch. 'How time flies,' he said. 'Fred will be watching out for you. You'd better be off, Alfie.'

Mr Brock opened the door. Alfie took the hint and, with a flick of his tail, disappeared down the passage.

'Our Alfie's turned up like a bad penny,' cried Hack when Alfie arrived at the station.

'Like a very good penny,' Fred corrected, as he bent down and tickled the railway cat. 'Passengers have been enquiring about you, Alfie. Ready for breakfast?'

'Miaow!' said Alfie. Thank you. Two breakfasts are always better than one!

The station was very busy. So many trains to meet, just as many to see away and parcels to be handled. To and fro over the bridge went Alfie all day. Fred was shutting the main gate after the last train had departed, when a very tired cat ran past him.

'Hey, Alfie, come back!' yelled Fred. 'Where are you off to now?'

'Miaow!' cried Alfie over his shoulder. I'm going to keep guard with Mr Brock of course.

The rocking-horse mender was just about to lock up for the night when Alfie appeared. 'Thought you'd come along,' said Mr Brock. 'I'm very glad to see you, but I do hope we sleep soundly tonight.'

Once in bed it didn't take them long to fall fast asleep as the horses kept watch round them, and nothing disturbed them that night.

# 3

# Hack is Worried

After a good night's sleep Alfie felt ready for anything. He left Mr Brock's early and ran back to the station to be first on duty.

Hack came next and unlocked the staff-room door. 'Hungry, eh, Alfie?' he asked as he went to the cupboard. 'Won't keep you waiting long.'

Alfie blinked in surprise. Hack had evidently heeded Fred's stern words about his behaviour. The Leading Railman was polite to everyone all morning. In fact, it was a pleasure to work alongside him, thought Alfie, as he bustled about among the passengers.

About midday two men, last to leave a train from London, stopped to speak to Hack at the gate. They asked many questions about passengers and traffic. Hack was very civil but was reluctant to answer so many queries. He looked round for Fred, who was not in sight.

'Miaow?' said Alfie as he stared hard at the men. Why do you want to know so much about our railway?

At last one of the men glanced cautiously over his

shoulder before speaking. 'Confidentially,' he began in a whisper, 'we are part of the railway fraud squad . . .'

'Miaow!' interrupted Alfie, alarmed. No need to take *my* paw marks, I've done nothing wrong.

'. . . looking out for fare dodgers and other criminals.'

'Oh well, that's different,' said Hack relieved.

'For instance,' the man continued, 'have you handled any freight lately that might attract attention?'

'No, I don't think so,' said Hack, 'just the usual mail bags and parcels.' He thought for a moment. 'There's Rex, of course, the valuable old rocking-horse Mr Brock is mending.'

'Really? How interesting. We won't miss the opportunity of visiting Mr Brock. Where does he live?' said the other man.

'Miaow!' cried Alfie, who had taken an instinctive dislike to both men. Don't tell them, Hack!

But to Alfie's dismay Hack gave the men precise directions to the rocking-horse mender's workshop.

'Thank you,' said the first man. 'We won't forget to mention your name at Headquarters for being courteous and helpful. You might even get promotion.'

Hack looked very pleased with himself. The men set off and after them went Alfie. Arriving opposite Mr Brock's, the men stared at the house as they strolled past. From a nearby doorway Alfie watched as they turned and walked back, stopping to take a longer look at the house and peering down the passage. Then they nodded to one another as if in satisfaction and returned to the village.

Now why hadn't they visited Mr Brock as they had said they would, thought Alfie? He felt very uneasy all afternoon and he kept out of the way when Hack saw the men off on the early evening London train. Alfie hoped he'd never see either of them again.

Determined not to leave Mr Brock on his own for one single night while Rex was with him, Alfie went along to the workshop after the last train had left the station. 'I don't know what I'd do without you,' said Mr Brock as he opened the door for Alfie. 'But don't keep scratching the door. Just miaow. I'll hear you.'

It wasn't long before they were both in bed. Mr Brock fell asleep almost as soon as his head touched the pillow, but Alfie was fidgety, and moonlight streaming in through the window kept him awake. He jerked his head at every slight sound and he wriggled about constantly.

At last the old man opened his eyes and said, 'Oh, *please*, Alfie, lie still or neither of us will have a wink of sleep all night.'

Alfie didn't move for a while but he stayed on the alert. Then, just as he was dozing off, he heard a faint noise outside. Someone moving about? Cautiously he raised his head and saw a shadow pass the window. He waited, trembling. Whoever it was returned and stared into the workshop.

'Miaow!' said Alfie quietly, as he crawled up the bed and pawed Mr Brock's shoulder. The old man refused to move, so Alfie pulled at his pyjama jacket until he opened one eye.

'Oh, dear, what's the matter now, Alfie?' he sighed. He raised himself on one elbow and as he was facing the window, immediately caught sight of the figure outside.

Resourcefully, he picked up a thick stick which was lying on the floor beside the bed. 'I'm ready for anyone who dares enter my workshop,' he whispered as, followed by Alfie, he crept across the floor towards the door. The figure at the window had disappeared. Mr Brock clutched the stick as he and Alfie stood behind the door and listened. There was silence.

'Probably just some petty thief slinking about,' said Mr Brock after a time. 'I'll report the matter to the police tomorrow. We might as well lie down again.'

He turned towards the bed, but suddenly there were sounds of a struggle outside and they heard a shout, 'Got you!'

'That's Constable Pringle's voice!' cried Mr Brock. 'He promised to keep a special watch on my premises.'

The scuffle outside continued. 'I must go to his aid,' shouted Mr Brock. He unlocked the door and darted

out brandishing the stick. Alfie peered round the door-way and saw two forms, one in uniform, locked in a struggle.

Mr Brock joined in the fray. He lifted the stick high towards the intruder and, missing his aim, caught the policeman a glancing blow on the side of his head.

'Miaow!' howled Alfie as Constable Pringle went down like a ninepin. Now you've done it, Mr Brock. Striking a policeman – a *real* crime! And you've knocked off his hat as well.

To Alfie's relief, the constable, holding his head, got

swiftly to his feet and cried out, 'Catch him, Mr Brock –
don't let him get away!'

The rocking-horse mender swung round and
grabbed the man who, strangely, had not attempted to
run off. 'I'm holding him,' shouted Mr Brock. Alfie ran
out of the workshop and joined the group. For the first
time they all got a good view of the man in Mr Brock's
grasp.

'Why! Would you believe it? It's *Hack*!' gasped the
rocking-horse mender.

'Miaow!' said Alfie. So it is!

'May I ask what you are doing here?' asked Constable
Pringle severely.

Hack looked very embarrassed. 'Well, er . . . thinking about it afterwards, I was worried about the intentions of two men who asked a lot of questions at the
station this morning,' he said, trembling. 'So I came
along just in case Mr Brock needed help.'

'It's not your job to keep watch on Mr Brock,' said
the constable, 'and in any case you are trespassing on
private property.'

'I'm sure Hack had my interests at heart,' said Mr
Brock. He looked nervously at the bump which had
appeared on the constable's head. 'And, my goodness,
I didn't intend hitting *you*, Constable. It was all a
mistake.'

'Never mind about that now,' said the constable. 'It's all in the course of duty.' He picked up his hat.

'Shall we go inside?' suggested the rocking-horse mender.

In the workshop the three men talked things over, while Alfie listened. Constable Pringle said it was his duty to report the matter, but he was sure that, in the circumstances, a lenient view would be taken of Mr Brock striking a policeman and of Hack prowling round in the middle of the night.

'But don't do such a stupid thing again, Hack,' warned the constable. '*We'll* look after Mr Brock, there's no need for you to interfere.'

'I'm very lucky,' said Mr Brock. 'Police keeping guard outside, and Alfie inside for company.'

Eventually the constable and Hack departed and Mr Brock and Alfie went back to bed, only to toss and turn for what was left of the night.

Next morning back at the station Alfie found Hack going about his duties with a worried, resentful expression on his face. Not for the first time Alfie felt sorry for him. He was sure that Hack had only acted out of concern for the rocking-horse mender.

Later on Alfie was relieved when he overheard Fred telling Hack that the police had decided to overlook the little matter of trespassing by Hack, and the more serious one of Mr Brock hitting a policeman.

'But, for goodness sake, Hack, pull yourself together and let's have no more nonsense of this sort,' said Fred. 'I'll be in the office if you want me.' Off he went.

It was quiet on the station and Hack sat down on a platform seat. Alfie jumped up on to the seat and sat down beside him. The railway cat was surprised when Hack started to talk to him. 'Fact is, Alfie,' he said. 'I never know when I'm doing the right thing.'

'Miaow!' said Alfie. I know *exactly* how you feel!

Hack absently stroked Alfie. Then he put a hand into a pocket and pulled out a ping-pong ball. Alfie looked up at Hack, then down at the ball. Could it be possible? Was Hack really going to play games?

'Found this in a compartment,' said Hack. 'Catch, Alfie!' He threw the ball right to the top of the bridge steps. Alfie sprang up as if released from a catapult, and was up the steps in no time at all. He followed the ball as it bounced down, step by step, on to the platform where he had a strenuous time trying to catch it. When he did manage to touch the ball he found he couldn't hold on to it and off it went, bouncing along the platform.

'Miaow!' said Alfie looking up at Hack, who was laughing at the railway cat's antics.

Hack bent down and picked up the ball. He was

about to throw it up the steps again when the first passenger for the next train arrived. Hack hastily put it into his pocket. 'Another time, Alfie,' he whispered.

'Miaow!' said Alfie. I'm very glad to know you can play games.

# 4

# Ghost-ridden!

Alfie continued to spend nights with Mr Brock and he often popped into the workshop during the day.

'Like a cat on hot bricks, our Alfie,' said Hack. 'Here one minute, off to Mr Brock's the next.'

'Alfie is rather restless,' admitted Fred. 'He probably senses our concern about Rex's safety. Cats are remarkable creatures.'

'You can say that again!' cried Hack.

'It seems to me rocking-horses are very much in the news at present,' Fred went on. 'For instance, those two men you told me about who asked a lot of questions. I've made enquiries and they were certainly not railway detectives. Very strange.'

'I know I shouldn't have told them anything,' said Hack hastily. 'You warned me not to behave like a detective, but I can't help keeping my ears and eyes open all the time.'

'Quite right. Even Alfie's on the alert!' said Fred.

'Miaow!' agreed Alfie.

Alfie watched Hack as the Leading Railman closely studied every stranger who appeared at the station, and even stared hard at the regular passengers.

One man grumbled to Fred, 'Why is Hack acting as if he suspects one of us might have the crown jewels stuffed under our jacket?'

Fred laughed. 'Oh, take no notice,' he said. 'We've all got something on our minds at present.'

One day on arriving at the workshop Alfie found Mr Brock very upset. 'Alfie,' said the old man. 'I'm convinced someone has been in my workshop without permission. Earlier this morning I locked the door and secured the window before going out for a short while. When I came back I found my brushes and tools had been tampered with.'

'Miaow!' said Alfie alarmed.

He glanced up at the window. 'Miaow!' he said again. No one, except me, could squeeze through that ventilator.

'How did someone get in? And out again?' said Mr Brock. 'It's ghostly! But, thank goodness, Rex hasn't been harmed.' He sighed. 'How I shall miss that horse, but how relieved I shall be to see him safely on his way. Ah well, back to work.'

The old man reached up and took down a tin of primer from a shelf. 'There's very little more work to be

done on Rex,' he said. 'I hope to give him the final touches before the week is out.'

'Miaow!' said Alfie. That means only a few more days of anxiety.

Just then there was a knock on the door. They both jumped. In walked the postman. 'Whatever's the matter?' he asked as he caught sight of the startled look on Mr Brock's face.

'I'm almost distracted,' said Mr Brock, and he told the postman what had happened, adding, 'but no damage has been done and, so far as I can tell, nothing has been stolen.' He shook his head. 'It's a mystery.'

'Well, if it's Rex you're worried about,' said the postman, 'it's my opinion that it would be very difficult for anyone to steal him and eventually sell him without being traced.'

'That's true,' sighed Mr Brock. 'But there are some very clever, dishonest, people about nowadays. When I was a lad . . .'

'Yes, yes, Mr Brock,' interrupted the postman hastily. 'I know. It was different then. Sorry I can't stay for a chat, but I've a very large round today. See you tomorrow.' He waved to Alfie as he went out.

Mr Brock worked hard for the rest of the day and Alfie stayed with him most of the time. Sleep didn't come easily that night as they lay on the camp-bed. Had someone really managed to break into the workshop while Mr Brock was out? If so, what could he, or she, be interested in, if not Rex?

Alfie was relieved when the first grey light of dawn shone through the window. He was back early at the station. He found passengers and staff content because trains were running to time and everything looked neat and tidy. For once, the platforms had been properly swept by Hack.

Fred came on duty. 'Hello, Alfie,' he said. 'How is Mr Brock getting on with Rex?'

'Hope he won't take much longer,' Hack put in, 'or we'll all be nervous wrecks.'

'Not as bad as that, surely?' laughed Fred. He held out a parcel. 'Hack, will you please take this along to the workshop. Mr Brock's waiting for it.'

Hack set off with the parcel and Alfie followed. Mr Brock greeted them at the workshop door. He was more disturbed than Alfie had ever seen him. 'Someone has been in *again*!' he cried.

'Have you informed the police?' asked Hack.

'I mentioned the matter to Constable Pringle when he called yesterday,' was the answer.

'Well, I should get in touch with him again, immediately,' said Hack.

'I'll take your advice,' said the rocking-horse mender. 'Will you please stay on guard with Alfie while I go and phone from the house?' He was already half-way down the passage.

'Don't worry, Rex will be in safe hands so long as I'm about,' Hack called after him. Hands in pockets he stood just outside the door and kept turning his head from side to side as he kept a sharp look-out.

Alfie suddenly pricked up his ears as he heard a slight sound from inside the workshop. He glanced quickly at Hack, who had obviously heard nothing. Quickly Alfie streaked into the workshop. He stopped short for, standing by Rex, were two dirty-looking children, a boy and a girl.

The children giggled and hunched their shoulders when they saw Alfie. 'Sssh!' said the boy with finger to lip.

Alfie's tail flicked as Mr Brock's footsteps were heard approaching. With a whispered, 'Let's have a bit of fun, shall we?' the boy started to push Rex vigorously. The girl joined in. Backwards and forwards went the horse, rearing higher and higher until he appeared to Alfie to be in danger of rocking right over.

Then the children rushed across the workshop and squeezed behind the crate standing in a corner. Just as Hack was about to step inside, Alfie ran after the children and pushed in between their legs. He poked his head round the side of the crate.

Hack strolled in, stopped in his tracks, gasped and put a hand to his mouth. His eyes widened in fright as he stared at Rex still rocking violently.

'Ahh . . . ahh . . . ahh . . .' he yelled as he turned back and nearly knocked Mr Brock over.

'Hey, look where you're going, Hack!' protested the old man. 'What's the trouble?'

Hack gulped. 'This pl . . . pl . . . place must he haun . . . haun . . . haunted,' he stammered. 'Look!'

Apprehensively Mr Brock peered into the workshop. 'Rex is rocking . . .' he began in amazement.

'. . . On his own!' Hack pointed out. *'He's being ridden by a ghost!* Let's scram.'

But Mr Brock grasped his arm. 'Non . . . nonsense, Hack,' he said, in a trembling voice. 'There must be a rational explanation.' They watched for a few seconds, then Mr Brock cried, 'He's slowing down.'

'Th . . . th . . . that's because we're looking at him,' said Hack.

At that moment Mr Brock caught sight of two round bright eyes staring at him. 'There's Alfie behind the crate!' he exclaimed.

'Oh! Might have guessed that cat would have a paw in this,' cried Hack exasperated. 'Wouldn't surprise me if any minute he swished past us on a broomstick.'

Still holding on to Hack, Mr Brock led the way towards the corner. As they crept nearer they heard a muffled sound. Both men dashed forward and pulled the crate away from the wall. And there crouched the children. Before they could escape Mr Brock grabbed the boy, and Hack the girl.

'Who are you?' asked Mr Brock as he shook the boy slightly.

'I'm Robin,' was the reply, 'and she's my sister, Sara.

We're twins and we've come to live at the bottom of your garden.'

'Really?' said Mr Brock. He turned to Hack. 'I've been so busy working on Rex I haven't had time even to enquire about my new neighbours.'

'But how did you manage to get in?' Hack wanted to know.

'Easy,' said Robin. He pointed at the old-fashioned disued fireplace. 'Down there. It's wide and there are plenty of bricks sticking out to use as handholds and footholds.'

'Well I never!' cried an astonished Mr Brock as he gazed at the twins. 'And it's very dirty in there.'

Sara broke in eagerly. 'We wanted so much to see Rex as we had heard people talking about him, but we were ordered not to bother you.'

Mr Brock smiled. 'Well, I can understand you wanting to have a look at the old horse, but you must ask my permission *first*.' He pushed the children forward. 'Here are your ghosts, Hack.'

'Oh, they didn't fool *me*,' said Hack loudly. 'I was only joking about the workshop being haunted.'

Mr Brock smiled again and Alfie cried, 'Miaow!' Oh, no, you weren't joking!

'Would you like a ride on Rex?' Mr Brock asked the children.

'Please!' they cried in unison.

'And Alfie?' said Sara.

Robin and Sara climbed on to Rex's back. 'Now Alfie,' said Mr Brock as he lifted the railway cat and placed him in front of the twins. 'Rex is strong enough to carry you all,' he said proudly.

The door opened and in came Constable Pringle. 'Ho – ho!' he cried, surprised. 'What's going on? I thought you were in trouble, Mr Brock.'

'Oh, I'm sorry to have bothered you, Constable,' said Mr Brock as he continued to push Rex. 'It was a false alarm.'

'Well, we're certainly getting used to those,' said the constable.

After the ride the children were sent off home – through the workshop door!

That night before going to sleep Alfie glanced at Rex bathed in moonlight, with the other rocking-horses all round him. Just then Alfie couldn't really blame Hack for believing in ghosts . . .

# 5

# A False Alarm

Twice next day Alfie caught sight of the twins peeping round the door watching Mr Brock at work.

'Miaow!' cried Alfie loudly on the second occasion. Go away. Stop disturbing Mr Brock.

The old man looked up and the children scampered away. He shook his head. 'Very mischievous children,' he said. 'I'll have to keep everything under lock and key, in case they get in here again unobserved.'

'Miaow!' said Alfie. I'll keep an eye on them for you. He followed the children home and squatted down outside the cottage. The twins' mother noticed him.

'That's a very fine-looking cat,' said Mrs Tucker.

'He's the station cat,' Robin told her.

'He's a magnificent cat,' added Sara.

Alfie stretched out, bent his head and rolled right over. Mrs Tucker invited him inside and gave him a slice of chicken. Alfie enjoyed all the fuss, but he didn't trust the children out of his sight for the rest of the day.

His vigil didn't cease when darkness fell. He

wouldn't put it past the rascals sneaking out of the house when their parents were asleep. After a quick dash back to the station for supper, he returned to his post.

When the last light went out in the cottage the railway cat made his way via a shed roof to the window sill outside the twins' bedroom. The curtains were drawn and the window partly open.

To pass the time profitably Alfie kept a sharp look-out for anything moving. Once he crouched right down when he thought he saw a fox slinking across the garden, but it turned out to be a farm dog. Alfie stayed quite still for at least an hour, but the dog didn't return. Suddenly he became aware of movements inside the bedroom. He got to his feet when light from a torch flickered through the curtains.

The twins must be getting out of bed!

Putting his left ear close to the window pane Alfie heard whispering. 'Now's our best chance while they're asleep,' said Robin. 'We'll get the scissors and cut it up straight away before they can stop us.'

Alfie did not catch all of the rest of the conversation, but he did hear Sara mention Rex, and then giggle.

Alfie flattened his ears and growled in his throat. Cut it up? he thought. What? Surely they didn't intend damaging the old horse. Unthinkable! Yet there

was something afoot and Rex might be harmed
unintentionally.

Desperately Alfie started jumping against the
window. He heard Sara gasp, but Robin said, 'It's all
right, silly. I guess it's only Alfie.'

He drew back the curtains and stuck his head out of
the window. 'Sshh, Alfie!' he whispered. 'We've got a
job on hand, so be a good cat and leave us alone.'

Gently he pushed until Alfie was forced to jump

down. How undignified! Alfie was furious at such treatment. He sat down outside the front door and waited uneasily for the twins to emerge with the scissors.

But nothing happened.

Mystified, he waited until sunrise before he ran back to the workshop, to be let in by Mr Brock. 'I've missed you, Alfie,' said the old man. 'Have you been out all night?'

'Miaow!' said Alfie. I've been on guard duty. He accepted a cod's head and some milk before deciding to pay a brief visit to the station.

A second breakfast provided by Hack did nothing to calm his fears. Cut it up? Cut it up? kept going through his mind. Without staying even to wash himself he started off again, but Hack caught hold of his tail.

'Think Mr Brock can't manage without you, you conceited cat?' said the Leading Railman scornfully. 'Well, let me remind you, your job is to keep the vermin down on this station.' He grabbed Alfie and shut him in the staff room.

Alfie howled and howled until Fred came on duty and released him. Fred started to advise him, 'Now then, Alfie, Hack's got a point, you *are* the station cat and . . .'

But before Fred could move, the railway cat streaked

between the man's legs and was off like a shot. Mr Brock was surprised to see him back so soon.

'I'll be unpopular with the station staff for keeping you away from your station duties!' he exclaimed.

'Miaow!' cried Alfie. You might need the help of an intelligent cat like me soon!

There was no sign of the children during the morning. After lunch Alfie sat down and watched Mr Brock at work. He tried hard to keep alert, but his eyes closed, his head sank on to his chest and he fell asleep.

But he woke immediately when he heard someone outside the workshop. Robin's head appeared round the door.

Alfie sprang up and cried, 'MIAOW!'

Mr Brock looked up startled. 'What's the matter, Alfie?' he said. 'If those twins are lurking round here again, I'll have to think what to do with them!'

He waited for a while and then resumed work. After a time he put down his tool and told Alfie, 'Just going round to the back for cleansing fluid. You'll be in charge for exactly one minute.'

As soon as the rocking-horse mender's back was turned, Alfie was alarmed, but not surprised, when the twins rushed into the workshop. They each carried a bundle under one arm. They ran up to Rex. Robin quickly draped what appeared to be a tatty woollen

271

cloth on top of the horse's head, while Sara pressed something similar on to his rump.

Mr Brock entered and stopped in amazement as he gazed at the horse.

'We thought Rex ought to have a new mane and tail,' Robin said eagerly, 'so we've made them specially for him.'

'I do hope you are pleased, Mr Brock,' said Sara anxiously.

Speechless, Mr Brock walked all round Rex, while the children stood by, beaming. 'Well . . .' he began at last, as he stroke his chin. 'It was . . . er . . . a very kind thought, but –'

Alfie jerked his head round as he heard someone enter the workshop. Mrs Tucker came forward. She stared at Rex. Her eyes glinted and her face was flushed. Alfie could tell that she was very annoyed. She might explode! The children backed away as she pointed at Rex.

'That's my *rug*!' she cried. (So *that's* what it is, thought Alfie.)

'But it's only an old rug,' wailed Sara, beginning to cry.

'Indeed it is,' said Mrs Tucker. 'It belonged to your great-grandmother.'

'I'm sure the children meant well,' said Mr Brock

hastily. He turned to Robin. 'Have you kept the rest of the rug pieces?' he asked.

Robin nodded.

'Well then,' said the rocking-horse mender, 'I've got some very strong needles and, as soon as I've finished work on Rex, you two can help me sew the pieces together again. The old rug will look as good as new.'

The corners of Mrs Tucker's mouth started to twitch.

'That's very kind of you, Mr Brock,' she said. 'I'll agree, on condition that my children promise to be on their best behaviour for at least a month.'

The twins promptly apologized to Mr Brock and promised to behave for one month. But Alfie didn't believe they'd manage even for one *day*!

Then Mrs Tucker invited the rocking-horse mender, and the railway cat, to join the family for a cream tea at the cottage. As they were leaving the workshop Mr Brock turned to look at Rex.

'I must say, Rex is very handsome with his makeshift mane and tail,' he exclaimed.

'Miaow!' cried Alfie. What a fib, Mr Brock!

Anyhow, another alarm over, thought Alfie. What would tomorrow bring?

# 6

# Another Scare

There was an air of excitement about the station as news that Mr Brock had almost completed work on Rex spread. Passengers talked about the horse.

'I must pop into the workshop to see Rex before he leaves,' said one.

'You'll have to give Rex a good send-off, Fred.'

'Mr Brock's going to miss him.'

'Alfie is sure to miss him too.'

'It's funny how that horse has caught people's imagination,' said Hack.

'Not funny at all,' said Fred. 'They all realize he's unique.'

It was half-term holiday and train-spotters were out in force. Clutching note books and pens or pencils they stood in small groups at the far end of the platforms, checking numbers as trains passed.

Once or twice Alfie noticed a man, dressed in a long black coat with a velvet collar, striding about the station. The man wasn't interested in train-spotting, but looked intently at everything on the station, even at the posters on the walls.

Alfie thought he looked a jolly sort of man so he started following him round. The man seemed glad of Alfie's company. Once he stopped and bent down to have a word with the railway cat. 'I think this station will do very nicely,' he said.

'Miaow!' said Alfie. Nicely for what?

After a time Alfie made his way to the booking office. He found Hack talking to Brown.

'I can't understand why that man is spending so much time at our station,' said Hack. 'It looks very suspicious to me.'

'Oh, come off it, Hack!' cried Brown. 'You'll be accusing that little old lady who stepped off the last train of having designs on Rex. I've already said, if the man had been interested in the old rocking-horse, he would have made straight for Mr Brock's instead of spending so much time here.'

Hack shook his head. 'I'm not taking any chances,' he said stubbornly. 'Fred doesn't want to be disturbed this morning, but all the same I'm going to interrupt him and ask his advice.'

'Miaow!' said Alfie quietly. I'm sure you're wrong about the man.

Alfie followed Hack into Fred's office. After he had

listened to Hack, Fred said, 'Oh dear! I'm sorry you've been bothered, Hack. I forgot to inform you that we were expecting a special visitor today. He's a famous television producer, who wants to use our station as a location for a new film.'

Alfie miaowed with relief and pleasure at this news.

'Hello, old chap,' said Fred. 'Didn't notice you. I'm sure the railway cat will be needed in the film. You might earn enough money for extra fish and cream. What do you think of that?'

'Miaow!' cried Alfie as he jumped up at Fred's legs. I think I will make an exceptionally good actor!

'You'd better get along, Hack, and see if the producer needs any assistance. Tell him I'll join him when I've finished this urgent job.'

Alfie decided he had left Mr Brock on his own long enough. He turned to go, but halted in the doorway. His nose quivered and his tail twitched.

'What's the matter, Alfie?' asked Fred. He sniffed. 'Something's burning!' he yelled as he got hastily to his feet and made for the door.

As they all rushed out on to the platform they could see a cloud of smoke over the village.

'It's coming from the far end,' shouted Hack.

'Oh no!' cried Fred. 'It can't be. It couldn't *possibly* be . . . !'

Alfie hesitated no longer. He was off like an arrow from a bow. Don't panic, he told himself. The fire might not be at Mr Brock's after all.

His way was blocked by a small group of people who coughed and spluttered as dense smoke from burning fat rose higher in the air. With eyes smarting, Alfie slipped between a forest of human legs to find smoke and flames pouring out of the fish and chip shop, which was only three doors away from the rocking-horse mender's workshop!

Alfie caught sight of the owner of the shop, and his

wife, watching helplessly as the firemen got busy with hoses. He was glad when he heard someone call out, 'No one's been hurt!' (But Alfie could hardly bear the thought of all that lovely fish going up in smoke!)

The railway cat got a thorough drenching as he shot past the firemen. He found Mr Brock standing in front of his house watching the commotion.

The old man was shaking. 'It's all right now, Alfie,' he called out in a quavering voice. 'I was just about to drag Rex out of the workshop in case the fire spread when a fireman called to tell me there is no danger as the fire is now under control.'

He mopped his forehead with a handkerchief. 'I've shut the door and window to keep out the smoke. It would be terrible if Rex was damaged just when he's nearly ready to leave. Really, I never know what's going to happen next!'

Alfie, purring loudly, weaved in and out of Mr Brock's legs.

'My word, you are wet!' exclaimed the old man. 'Come inside.'

As he rubbed Alfie down with an old towel, Mr Brock said, 'Tuesday's my fish and chip day, so there'll be very little lunch for us today I fear.'

But he was wrong. At that moment a neighbour came down the passage and into the workshop. 'I've got a nice big cottage pie in my oven, Mr Brock,' she said. 'I'll bring some along in half an hour or so, and there'll be a portion for Alfie as well.'

'Prrr . . . rrr . . . rr . . .' went Alfie. He had sampled Mrs Morris's cottage pies on previous occasions.

'That's very neighbourly of you, Mrs Morris,' said Mr Brock.

The fire at the fish and chip shop was almost extinguished by the time Mrs Morris reappeared with the cottage pie.

'Eat it while it's hot,' she said. She stopped on her way out to gaze at Rex. 'I can't take my eyes off that horse when I come in here,' she said. 'He's such a handsome animal.'

'You won't be seeing him much longer, Mrs Morris,' said the rocking-horse mender sadly.

'Well, Mr Brock, you've got plenty of other work to occupy you,' said Mrs Morris briskly. 'Those two over there for instance.' She pointed to two old dappled-grey fairground horses which were in very poor condition.

'Oh yes,' said Mr Brock, brightening up. 'I've got hours and hours of work on those two.'

With many thanks from Mr Brock and purrs from Alfie, Mrs Morris left them to their meal. The cottage pie was excellent. Afterwards Mr Brock lay down on the camp-bed and Alfie curled up alongside him. 'Prrr . . .

rrr . . . rrr . . .' he sang as Mr Brock tried to doze off.

The old man raised his head to look down at Alfie. 'Really, Alfie!' he laughed. 'You keep me awake in the daytime as well as at night!'

Alfie tried to stay still as he gazed at Rex. During the past few weeks Alfie had watched Mr Brock performing expert 'surgery' on Rex. The day arrived when the last coat of paint had been put on, after which Mr Brock had dabbed large black spots on Rex's body and painted a white diamond on his forehead. When the paint had dried, Rex had been fitted with a new leather saddle and bridle and gleaming brass stirrups.

It was obvious to Alfie that Rex's transformation was almost complete. Soon the old rocking-horse would be seen safely off at the station – and there would be nothing more for Alfie to worry about.

# 7

# Alfie is taken for a Ride

Mr Brock rose early next morning. Alfie stretched out and clenched and unclenched his claws before rolling over and falling off the camp-bed.

Mr Brock laughed. 'Come on, sleepy-head,' he said, 'this is an important day. First breakfast, then I'll finish work on Rex.'

'Miaow!' cried Alfie. Feeling very excited he joined the rocking-horse mender for breakfast in the house. Back in the workshop after the meal, Mr Brock walked around the old horse and studied him from every angle. 'There's only one more job to be done,' he announced. 'What's that, Alfie?'

'Miaow!' sang Alfie. He's minus mane and tail, of course.

'A new mane and tail for Rex,' said Mr Brock, smiling.

He picked up some long black horsehair, and made a mane for the horse, shaping it to fit down the neck. Then he cut some more horsehair for a tail. When these had been securely fixed and the rocking-horse mender could find nothing more to be done, he phoned the station and asked Fred to come along to the workshop.

Fred soon arrived, with Hack. 'I wasn't going to miss this,' said Hack.

'My word, Mr Brock, you have done a marvellous job,' said Fred as he stood back to admire the rocking-horse. He turned to Hack. 'Fit for a junk shop, did you say, Hack? Are you now prepared to eat your words?'

Hack grinned. 'All right, I'll have words for my supper tonight,' he said.

'I've enjoyed every minute of working on Rex,' said Mr Brock, 'and the thought of him leaving the country makes me shudder. I wouldn't mind so much if he was going back to his old home.'

'It's a shame he's got to be sold,' said Fred. 'But, whatever happens to him, I hope he will continue to give pleasure to children – and to grown-ups.'

'We'll all miss you, Rex,' said Hack as he gave the horse a friendly pat.

Fred looked at his watch. 'Time to go back to work,' he said. 'Day after tomorrow, Mr Brock, we'll collect Rex for his train journey to the auction rooms. In the meantime, it would be a good idea if you lined the bottom of the crate with more shavings.'

'I'll see to that,' promised Mr Brock as he opened the door for them. 'Staying, Alfie?'

'Miaow!' said Alfie. Please.

After breakfast next morning they returned to the workshop. Mr Brock examined the empty crate still standing in a corner. 'It does need more packing,' he said. He let down the side opening of the crate and started to bundle in shavings, sawdust and rolled-up papers. 'It wouldn't do to risk Rex being damaged in transit and spoiling all my hard work,' he said.

Alfie jumped into the crate and vigorously kneaded the packing with his paws. Then he curled up in the hollow he had made and looked up at Mr Brock.

'Miaow!' he said. It's very comfortable in here.

'Come out of there, Alfie,' laughed Mr Brock. 'We don't want to lose you as well as Rex.' Alfie pushed his nose right down between his paws. 'Now then, you heard me. Out you come,' coaxed Mr Brock.

Alfie was just about to oblige when there was a sharp rap on the door and two men, both in overalls, entered the workshop. Alfie stayed where he was.

'Good morning, Mr Brock,' said one man.

Alfie peeped out of the crate and immediately recognized the men who had asked Hack so many questions, and whom Alfie had observed walking slowly past Mr Brock's. This could be catastrophic, thought the railway cat!

'There's been a change of plan,' the man continued.

'The old rocking-horse is wanted at the auction rooms a day earlier, so instead of going by rail tomorrow we have been ordered to transport him by road *today*.'

Mr Brock looked bewildered as the man handed him a document. 'Here you are,' he said 'Authority to collect one antique rocking-horse, name of Rex.'

The rocking-horse mender glanced at the paper. 'This seems to be in order,' he said slowly, 'but Fred didn't say anything about it yesterday.'

'He didn't know about it then,' was the reply. 'Reason for the change of plan is that there will be a wealthy bidder at tomorrow's auction, and the horse must be there in good time.'

'I'd prefer to get in touch with Fred, if you don't mind,' said Mr Brock, in a flurry.

'No need for that,' said the man sharply. 'Please give us a hand with the crate. We've brought a truck along with us.'

Alfie, almost hidden by the packing, crouched in a corner of the crate as the loading took place. He only just managed to escape being flattened by the rockers. He shook with fright as the crate, with himself and Rex inside, was securely fastened, then wheeled down the passage and lifted into a waiting van.

One man jumped into the driving seat, the other into the passenger seat and within half a minute they were

off. Not for one moment did Alfie believe they were bound for the auction rooms. He had thought these men looked untrustworthy when he had first set eyes on them at the station, and he had been proved right. What would happen to Rex – and to Alfie himself?

Mr Brock had been duped. Somehow the robbers had managed to obtain all the information required for them to steal Rex at the right moment. With his ear towards a crack in the side of the crate, Alfie caught snatches of the men's conversation.

'That was a piece of cake!' laughed the driver.

'You're telling me,' said the other. 'We'll be at the

286

airport in record time. Soon this old rocking-horse will
be thousands of miles away, and we'll collect a generous
rake-off.'

Alfie felt trapped and helpless. The van was driven at
speed but occasionally had to slow down. When he
could, to relieve his tension, Alfie reached up and
clawed at a very small splinter of wood which he had
noticed underneath Rex's belly. After what seemed ages
the van suddenly pulled up with a jerk and Alfie fell
down flat.

'Keep calm, it's the police!' he heard the driver hiss to
his mate.

The rear van door was thrown open and someone –
must be a policeman, thought Alfie – climbed in and
called out, 'We're checking all vehicles.' Alfie jumped
as he heard a sharp rap on the side of the crate. 'What
have you got inside here?' said the policeman.

'A refrigerator,' was the driver's prompt reply.

'Well . . .' began the policeman.

He was interrupted by a voice from outside the van,
'You're wanted here for a moment, Sergeant.'

With an order, 'Switch off your engine,' the policeman jumped out of the van to join his colleague. At that
moment Alfie, in despair, hurled himself against the
side of the crate and, scratching frantically, howled and
howled.

'A refrigerator *howling*?' Alfie heard the policeman shout as he climbed back into the van. 'Let's see what you've really got in your van.'

The crate was unloaded on to the road. Alfie blinked when it was opened and he and Rex were revealed. He noticed first the two sullen men being held by police.

'Well, well, well,' said the first policeman. 'A rocking-horse and a cat.' He lifted the railway cat out of the crate. 'How did you get in there?' he asked.

'Miaow!' said Alfie. Rex and I were being taken for a ride.

'Does he belong to you?' asked the policeman turning to the robbers.

'No!' snarled one, with a baleful glance at Alfie.

'Fancy being caught because of a stupid cat,' said the other man.

'A very clever cat, you should say,' said the policeman. He stared at Alfie. 'I'm sure I've seen you before somewhere.'

Alfie purred. I've often been in the news, he wanted to tell him.

'We'll soon find out more about you, and the rocking-horse,' said the policeman.

Soon they were all at the police station. As Alfie lapped some milk he heard voices all around him, phones ringing and people coming and going. He

enjoyed his time in police custody. He was given plenty to eat and drink and was congratulated time after time for alerting the police.

Alfie wasn't in the least worried about getting back home. He'd been lost before, and Fred had always managed to find him. Sure enough, after several long telephone calls, the officer in charge came across to Alfie, who was sitting on a counter contentedly watching everything going on.

'We've traced your owners,' said the officer. 'You're Alfie, the railway cat.'

'Miaow!' said Alfie. Of course I am.

'I should have recognized you immediately, as I've seen your picture in the papers and on television. We could certainly do with a clever cat like you at *our* station,' he said.

'Miaow!' said Alfie hastily. Thank you, but Fred couldn't manage without me at *my* station.

Later that evening when Fred arrived, Alfie made a joyous rush at his friend. Fred scooped him up and squeezed him gently.

'Fine cat, that,' said the officer. 'Helped to catch two criminals who've been on the run for months. He can go home with you, but we'll have to keep the rocking-horse a little longer.'

'Well done, Alfie,' said Fred. The railway cat purred

contentedly as he sat upright in the front passenger seat of his friend's car and was driven back to the station.

In the staff room Alfie jumped up on to the comfortable chair, curled himself into a ball, put his chin on his tail and closed his eyes. Catching criminals was an exhausting job, he thought.

He opened one eye as he heard Fred lock the door behind him, but Alfie had no objection to being shut up in his own staff room. He was soon fast asleep.

# 8

# An Important Discovery

Next day everyone wanted to hear about the attempted robbery and Alfie's part in the rescue.

'If it hadn't been for Alfie, goodness knows where Rex would be by now,' said one passenger.

Others joined in, 'Alfie is always ready for any emergency.'

'He's almost human!'

Fred beamed at the railway cat, but Hack said, 'Oh, it's Alfie this and Alfie that. There's no end to hearing about that cat!'

Alfie purred louder to show his disdain for Hack's remarks.

'And, don't forget, clever as he is, Alfie hasn't solved the problem of keeping Rex in this country,' Hack went on. 'I don't suppose we'll ever see that horse again.'

Alfie stopped purring and Fred said solemnly, 'I'm afraid that's true.'

But they were wrong, for soon news came that Rex was being sent back to the workshop by rail, so that Mr Brock could examine him for possible damage.

Alfie made sure of being at the workshop when Rex arrived.

The rocking-horse mender started straight away on a thorough examination of Rex. To Alfie this seemed to take a long time. At last Mr Brock made a final check for any flaws by running his hand over the horse's smooth body surface.

'Well, Alfie,' he said. 'I think I can pass Rex as in perfect condition.' Then, 'Ouch! What's this?' he cried as he held up a blood-stained finger tip.

The old man bent down to look underneath the horse. 'Why! It's a splinter! However did I miss that? And *scratch* marks!'

Mr Brock looked hard at Alfie, who stared back at him. 'Oh, well, don't worry, Alfie,' he said. 'No real harm has been done. I'll soon repair it.'

A relieved Alfie jumped on to the platform underneath Rex, but the old man laughed as he gently pushed him aside. 'How do you expect me to do the repairs if you get in my way?' he said.

So Alfie sat on the floor. Mr Brock started by lightly sandpapering the scratched area. Suddenly he stopped, adjusted his spectacles and peered closer. 'And what's this?' he exclaimed. 'Would you believe it, there's a small crack as well. I really must have my eyesight tested.'

293

By this time Mr Brock was lying on his back underneath Rex. Alfie craned his neck, puzzled, as Mr Brock
picked up a penknife and carefully inserted it into the
crack. 'There's something wedged in the crack, Alfie,'
he cried excitedly.

Alfie moved closer as Mr Brock probed further and
eventually pulled out of the crack a folded-up piece of
yellowed paper. His face was flushed as he went over to
the bench and gently smoothed out the creases in the

paper. Then, with trembling hands, he held it up to the light.

'It's handwritten, Alfie,' cried the old man. 'Just listen to this.' He began to read as he peered at the faded lettering:

> *'This rocking horse has been made for,*
> *and belongs to, Susannah Jane Edmonds.*
> *23 April 1753.'*

He waved the paper at Alfie. 'Wonderful news, Alfie,' he cried. 'Wonderful.'

But Alfie couldn't understand why his friend should be so elated over a mere scrap of paper. Now if there had been a £50 note, or even a £5 note, inside Rex, that would have helped the family fortunes just a little, wouldn't it? It would have been better than nothing.

'How lucky that you scratched at Rex as you did, Alfie,' went on Mr Brock. 'This scrap of paper might never have been found but for you. Do you realize what an important document it is?'

'Miaow!' said Alfie. Not really, but I'm glad to be of use. Hope Hack hears about it.

'Rex is older than I had imagined, and so much more valuable,' said Mr Brock. He hesitated. 'And more likely to attract a foreign buyer with plenty of money, I suppose. But then, more money will help Rex's family, that's a comfort.'

The news about Rex travelled very quickly and next day the workshop was besieged with newsmen and cameramen. Fred and Hack came along as well. Much to Hack's annoyance Alfie was photographed at least half a dozen times with Mr Brock and Rex.

'Huh!' said Hack raising his eyebrows. 'That cat's at it again!'

'Say, "Miaow!" for us, Alfie,' urged a sound recordist.

But Alfie remained silent. *He* wasn't in the habit of miaowing to order for anyone.

'Obstinate cat, our Alfie,' said Hack.

'Miaow!' cried Alfie before he could stop himself. Stupid man, our Hack!

Eventually the excitement died down. One week passed and then another and nothing was heard about Rex's delivery to the auction rooms.

Mr Brock was hopeful and despondent by turns. He would mutter to himself and to Alfie. One day it would be, 'Perhaps the family will be able to keep Rex after all.' Another day he would say, 'They must be waiting for a very wealthy buyer to come forward.' Now and then, just for fun, Alfie jumped up on to Rex's back and, purring loudly, allowed Mr Brock to rock him to and fro.

One day when Alfie was in the workshop, they were

surprised by a visit from the Government official who had admired Rex. The man was very interested in the scrap of paper and wanted to hear firsthand about the discovery. Although he didn't understand everything

that was being discussed, Alfie listened intently as Mr Brock and the official held a long conversation.

After a time the man said, 'Well, Mr Brock, I will see what can be done about Rex. In my opinion that horse is a national heirloom and should remain in this country.'

He nodded to Alfie as he left the workshop. 'And that cat should be given a medal, or at least salmon suppers for a whole year!' he said smiling.

'Miaow!' cried Alfie as he followed the man to the door. You're a man after my own heart. I'll have the salmon, please.

Time passed and there was still no news about the fate of the rocking-horse, but one day Mr Brock came running to the station.

'Good news! Good news!' he shouted, as he tried to make himself heard above the noise of an outgoing train. When the train had left and silence reigned he went on, 'Everything's going to be all right. Rex is returning to his own home!'

'How's that?' asked Fred, as the staff and Alfie gathered round to listen.

'Our friend, the Government official, has used his influence to persuade an Historic Preservation Society to take the matter in hand,' Mr Brock said.

'Good for him,' said Fred.

Mr Brock smiled and nodded. 'I understand Rex's

owners are to be given an allowance so that they can continue living in the old mansion,' he said. 'One condition is that the house and gardens must be opened to the public on payment of an entrance fee.'

'That will help the family finances,' said Hack.

'Yes,' said Mr Brock. 'There will be many antique items for the public to view.'

'And Rex will be the principal attraction!' shouted Fred.

Everyone cheered and laughed as Mr Brock said, 'I'm sure he will. I'll have to get the crate ready again, but this time Rex will be going *home*.'

'By rail, I hope?' said Fred smiling.

'Of course!' said the rocking-horse mender. 'I wouldn't let him out of my workshop otherwise.'

'Miaow!' sang Alfie as he rolled over and over at Mr Brock's feet.

'Pity they can't take that cat as well. Put him on show,' said Hack.

'I'll make quite sure Alfie isn't shut inside the crate again,' said Mr Brock. 'In his own way he's just as valuable as Rex.'

When the time came for Rex's departure the station was thronged with people wanting to give him a good send-off. Alfie hung back as the guard blew his whistle and the train with Rex on board started to move slowly out of the station.

Now that Rex had gone everything seemed dull and uninteresting to Alfie. What should he do? He moped about the station until Fred said, 'Cheer up, for goodness sake, Alfie. You're making us all feel miserable.'

'And get on with a bit of mice catching. That's what you're here for,' cried Hack.

'Don't be hard on Alfie,' said Fred. 'Like all of us he's missing Rex. Pity we won't see that horse again.'

'And why not?' said Hack. 'We can pay to go and see him when he's put on show, same as anyone else, can't we?'

'That's the first sensible suggestion I've heard from you for a long time,' said Fred. 'A visit won't be possible just yet as I understand the house needs considerable improvement first. But I will organize an outing to go and see Rex on the very first day the house is open to the public.'

An outing to see Rex in his own home? thought Alfie, excited. That would be something to look forward to. Then a disturbing thought struck him. Would Fred be sure to include the railway cat on the outing?

'Miaow . . . Miaow . . .' he said anxiously as he looked up at Fred.

'What's the matter, Alfie?' said Fred. 'I promise we'll take you along, if that's what you're worrying about.'

Alfie was content. He knew that Fred would keep his promise.

And he did.

## DUSTBIN CHARLIE
### *Ann Pilling*

Charlie has always liked seeing what people threw out in their dustbins. So he's thrilled to find the toy of his dreams among the rubbish in the skip. But during the night, someone else takes it. The culprit in this highly enjoyable story turns out to be the most surprising person.

## CLASS THREE AND THE BEANSTALK
### *Martin Waddell*

Two unusual stories which will amaze you. Class Three's project on growing things gets out of hand after they plant a packet of Jackson's Giant Bean seeds. And when Wilbur Small is coming home, the whole street is buzzing – except for Tom Grice and his family, who are new in the street so don't know what the fuss is about, or why people are so nervous!

## THE TWIG THING
### *Jan Mark*

As soon as Rosie and Ella saw the house they knew that something was missing. It had lots of windows and stairs, but where was the garden? When they move in, they find a twig thing which they put in water on the window-sill, and gradually things begin to change.

## DODIE

### *Finola Akister*

Dodie the dachshund lives with Miss Smith and Tigercat in a country cottage. He has all sorts of adventures, because he's a very special dog. He is very good at finding things. He finds Miss Smith's key when she gets locked out, he finds Tigercat's new kitten, and he even finds a prickly hedgehog! Life is never dull for Dodie.

## HERE COME THE TWINS

### *Beverly Cleary*

Twins are full of surprises: just ask Mr Lemon, the postman. Janet and Jimmy can turn anything into a game, whether it's getting their first grown-up beds, or going to buy new shoes. But what will they do when their next-door neighbour gives them each a dog biscuit? Give them to a dog? No, that would be too easy!

## THE FRIDAY PARCEL

### *Ann Pilling*

Two highly enjoyable stories in which Matt goes to stay on his own with Gran-in-the-country, and sets his heart on buying a lion at the jungle sale.